Fragment

Acknowledgements

My boyfriend: Carlos Barraza

My friends: Leo, Keiko,

and of course you my lovely reader for picking up this book.

"This is how you do it: You sit down at the keyboard and you put one word after another until it's done. It's that easy, and that hard."

- Neil Gaiman

Sandra 1

Today is my special day. My dress is white as snow with a short three-foot train. Embroidered flowers fill the crown of the bust. I am beautiful, pure, and most importantly, innocent. Every noble in Lynxsis is in the room, gazing upon my groom and I. He is Klaud Demetri Bo, future King.

Klaud had a good reputation among the land. He and his family were always nice to us, and refreshingly not in the annoying, *I acknowledge your royal status* way. He was raised as a noble, so he understands what it's like to live up to expectations of others. He is a man that will soon be forever by my side; continuously knowing how to present himself in front of a crowd. He may not have been an actual King his entire life, but he was always a King at heart.

In a few moments, he would be my King.

We've been around each other our entire lives, so I don't think it was much of a shock when we announced our engagement. Then again, everything we did together had always been breathtaking.

Klaud looks at the perfectly placed diamond-encrusted veil sitting upon my Afro gold curls that were carefully pulled back into a high ponytail. I hope everyone likes the look. I play with my bouquet of blue hydrangeas. I cannot believe it's our wedding day.

My groom looks at me with his gleaming smile and sparkling gray eyes. He's beautiful. I can tell he feels the same way I currently do: nervous, heart pounding, fingers twitching. Yet, excited and ready to start a future together. Having kids, waking up next to each other and what-not. Lost in those short brown wavy curls he calls hair, I blush.

I wonder if everyone is enjoying the decorations. Some people still glance at them occasionally. Pearls and curtains made of the finest white silk draped every archway. The giant ice sculpture of Klaud and I standing within a heart, flowers blooming from the bottom. Some of the Nobles' children play with loose blue and purple orchid petals they picked up from the aisle. I see others stare at my three-tier chocolate wedding cake that is a few feet away from the orchestra.

This is it. Everything is in place. The orchestra is playing soft music. My father watches proudly with his light-brown eyes and bright white smile. Even from here I can tell his eyes are beginning to water. My mother, on the other hand, fights her smile. She never wants to show her true emotions; it's simply how she was raised.

In a matter of seconds our fate will be set in stone. Neither of us believe in divorce, so there is no going back. With this marriage, I will be officially recognized as Queen and Klaud will be King of the most powerful kingdom. Hopefully we will rule just as gracefully as my parents do, or even more so. Henceforth, they will be recognized as retired, or former Royals.

Impatience is approaching. *Could this wedding take any longer*? Let us be one already. We've been ready for this moment for years. Now that it's finally here, it seems like it's still taking an eternity.

As my thoughts end, the priest begins.

"Do you, Klaud, take our Queen of Lynxsis, Sandra Thorne, to be your loving wife? To have and to hold, in sickness and in health?"

"I do." Klaud responds.

"Do you, Sandra Thorne, take Klaud Demetri Bo as your husband? To not only be your husband, but also the King of Lynxsis?" the priest questions.

"I—"

The solid-oak double doors of the throne room are thrown open.

I am interrupted.

The doors crash thunderously into the walls. No announcement is made. Everyone's attention to the ceremony is broken. We instead focus on a man, decked in a full suit of silver armor, ride in on a white stallion. He pulls the reins, screeching to a stop, forcing it to stand on its hind legs. It bellows a neigh that echoes throughout the castle. Its mane flows wildly while a cacophonous sound erupts from steel horseshoes meeting white tile.

The moment, *my moment*, is lost...and never coming back.

"What is this madness?!" my father questions, jumping out of his seat.

He grabs his staff from my mother and strikes the ground with it repeatedly. Anger burning in his eyes. My mother stoically sits and waits, as usual. She believes everything happens for a reason, so she never reacts or speaks impulsively before a scenario plays out.

"Can't you see you are interrupting a once-in-a-lifetime ceremony?" father continues, "Two souls are being bound before the eyes of the Lord."

The intruder removes his helmet, revealing shoulder-length black curls and brown eyes. His hair settles as a deep exhale in exhaustion is let out.

"Forgive me, your Majesty. The Thornes have been summoned." he states.

"By who?" I shout. I'm bewildered and losing my composure.

"The guards at the Relic Center. I am the messenger. I'm here to tell you...*all of Magic is at stake*."

An unexpected response.

The guests gasp in shock. The report triggers whispers

amongst them. Turning to one another, completely forgetting about the ceremony. Glancing to my family with worried faces to illustrate their safety and peace is now our main priority. Do they not know whispering won't give them the peace they seek? That their gossip will only cause more problems? This will outweigh my wedding in no time; the worst news anyone can get. Now I'll be *the girl that barely had a wedding*. It'll be remembered as the day Magic was seemingly lost.

"Is that even possible?"

"I mean that's preposterous. There's no way."

Their whispers are getting louder.

"I'm afraid it is..." my father bellows, slamming his staff against the ground. "Attention! Calm yourselves. My daughter Sandra and I will appear at the Relic Center as the rightful representatives. As for this beautiful, grand wedding...it shall be placed *on hold* until we return from our trip. No one will speak of this announcement. To do so is punishable by *death*. My loving wife will oversee this, as well as protect you in my absence."

I cannot believe this. Today, *of all days*. Seconds away from marriage. All the planning and time...the precise decision making on guest lists, flowers, food, and seat placements...gone to waste. This could only happen to me. I swear, the life of a Royal is not what it's cracked up to be.

I pause my internal rage to take a deep breath. For generations I've always known my family to be cursed in regards to love. But never anything on this scale. Of course, we love our country, but when do we get *our* turn? Just a moment for us to have an untainted spotlight. I mean, sure, my parents made it. But I've always thought that it was just a fluke of sorts, a stroke of luck. Didn't think it could have happened again, until a few moments ago when everything was fine. Then this mad man crashed it. All my new hopes, shattered.

Couldn't the priest have given me two more minutes or was that too much to ask? I close my eyes and tilt my head upwards, facing the ceiling. *Kime veno ecrone.* This probably makes it look like a wish more than a begging prayer.

Finally, I turn to my maids and smile.

"Please prepare our things for departure to the Relic Center. We will need to leave immediately."

Honestly, Royals should be able to make quick work of something as simple as this. Or so I thought.

"We will be leaving by carriage." I add.

The maids scatter in their holy purple-and-green-accented uniforms to execute their orders. Eyes are scanning in every direction. The nobles at the Royals, the guest at the servants, and Klaud at me. I could barely wonder how he feels, my preoccupied stare with simmering resentment is towards my dad. His returned look could only be described as logical and, at most, two-percent genuinely apologetic.

The quelled whispers result in an air of awkward silence. Uneasy guests don't know what their next actions should be. The messenger, having accomplished his duties, dons his helmet and rides away through the same corridor he originated.

"You are free to depart to your homes." my dad announces to the attendees as he and I walk toward the entrance. Some of the lesser-known nobles get up and leave without hesitation. While others make sure the food doesn't go to waste.

This trip better not be in vain.

After about ten minutes, my father and I climb into the emergency carriage. It's nothing fancy at all. There are no jewels, no leather, no embroidery. Just horses to draw the carriage, a driver, a backseat with an overhang, and some type of side car we intended as a trunk. I guess it will have to do.

My mind begins to wander as the carriage takes off. *Oh, the life of a Royal; my curse.* My life constantly in danger, and paranoia is the norm. Not to mention, there always seems to be a problem that needs immediate attention. What will you spring upon us this time?

"Sandra," father whispers, "*matz nahavey*. I know you are disappointed and you wanted to have the perfect day. But you have duties to fulfill as a Royal. As a Queen."

"If you're trying to cheer me up father, it's not working. *As a Queen*? Due to an unfinished wedding, I'm still a Princess."

"Right..." he sighs.

My dad and I have a great relationship. But when it comes to ordeals like this, he'll always put Royal duties before anything. So, I bite my tongue.

"Well, I do not know what to say about the current circumstances. But I do know this: when all is said and done, Klaud will be waiting for you. And if you desire, we can redo your wedding on a grander scale."

What could I possibly say? Money nor status will ever get what I truly want. Yet, I can't have it. Even if I did, I would be disowned. No one would see me as elegant or pure. Certainly not innocent. I'm just playing the cards I was dealt.

"How about this:" my dad continues, "you can handle our *big problem* at the Relic Center. It can be your first act as Queen. Since it's the Relic Center, it will be sure to be worthy notoriety amongst nobles and subjects everywhere. Good introduction as Queen. Good for your image."

I perk up at the thought of doing my first act as Queen officially. Then my happiness fades to skepticism.

"Wait a minute," I begin, "are you just putting the work onto me? All so you can rush back to mom's side?"

Dad never likes leaving the throne nor my mother's side. He sticks to her like glue. *Is he trying to trick me?* His own daughter? Trying to lead me on by playing to my vulnerability. How dare he?

"What kind of father would I be if I did that?" he laughs. A clever one, I think.

Ari 2

I climb out of the carriage, dusting myself off while I straighten my traditional white-clad robe embroidered with gold near the bottom. The journey to the Relic Center took longer than I anticipated. How do they not expect their visitors to die of boredom on the trip? There's no sightseeing to be had. Before I can take my next breath, a disgruntled guard approaches me.

He stands tall in chainmail armor, shield and spear in hand. He squints his eyes, glaring, giving me a skeptical once-over. What? I get out of a pristine carriage, one of the best from Mardo, and that calls for him to give me the evil eye?

Is he jealous that I can afford such luxuries? Or is he wondering if I am the person he thinks I am? I do have quite the reputation, after all. Nonetheless, he should speak, before looking disgruntled with a person. It's simple manners. Or do they not teach such basic pleasantries to commoners in this part? I can't imagine there being much social interaction here.

"State your business here. Who are you?" the guard finally cracks his silence.

"I'm Ari Neclosse of Mardo. The abbot's right-hand man, if you will."

He just stands there looking at me. Does he not believe me? What's his issue? Is every visitor treated with this much respect? Or lack thereof. All he has to do is escort me; this talk is unnecessary. If this problem they summoned me for is as big a deal as they're claiming, how can we afford to be wasting time out in this blistering sun? No shade in sight. He may not care, but I take much pride in where I put my time and who I give it to. That being said, he's really not worth it. Plus, who is he to interrogate me?

"We were expecting the King himself for this matter. It's very dire." *He makes me wait just to say this?*

"The King gives his apologies; the Queen is terribly sick, and he must be there for her."

"Fine. I'll show you the problem, but I doubt you'll be able to fix it."

I may have been born a monk and raised a pacifist, but if he keeps this up, I will not hesitate to stab him with his own spear! I'd appreciate it if he kept his sly comments and judgmental looks to himself. I'm no commoner. I'm sure he wouldn't like half the things I could say about his low intellect and his obviously inferior position compared to mine. Who is he to make such inaccurate assumptions with as little as a glance? Oh, what I'd give to tell him a piece of my mind.

"Follow me." he says.

For the first time I realize how sandy it is. Little specks of red dust flying in the air cling to my attire as we walk toward the entrance. I miss the temple back home and our cool weather in the mountains already. It's all stacked stone and strong drafts of wind to keep us cool. And the view being much more than this grubby flatland in absolutely nowhere. I pick up my pace and continue following the guard.

We pass through automatic-sliding glass doors, immediately greeted by air conditioning that is a temperature below freezing. It seems I got what I asked for. We pass by approximately 14 guards in this corridor. I wonder how they endure this temperature? To stand here all day doing nothing in this a/c. Hopefully I can adjust as well as they did.

After a straight-shot down the hallway, we enter a room that opens into the shape of a dome. The room contains multiple white concrete pillars and a roof made of glass. I guarantee the night would allow me to see the galaxy in all its glory here. This spot would be absolutely perfect. After everything that's happened, I would *expect* this to be the most guarded room.

"Over there." The irritated guard says, pointing to an incubator.

I walk up to it cautiously. Inside are the most powerful Relics in the world. The heart of all Magic. A stone of citrine to represent fire, a lily to represent water, a feather for air, a wood-carved heart to represent earth, and a gold coin. The gold coin is to represent *Illusion Magic,* recognized as the purest and most valuable type of Magic. Forever these Relics shall float amongst each other in a circular motion.

I look closer and remember that they're supposed to be rotating the opposite way. Clockwise. So why the unexpected change in direction? This is troublesome indeed. These Relics have been here before time itself. Why is this happening? And what exactly do these guards expect us to do about it?

I step back from the incubator with a freshly troubled mind. I let out a huff and spot a woman when I look up. A woman of my age. Someone I have only heard of. Someone I could only *dream* of laying eyes on. Could it really be her standing in the same room as me?

Drenched in dark attire, she leans against the wall unaccompanied. Her black cape with light fur lining stops just before it hits the floor. Jet-black hair, deep-green eyes. She's cold inside and out. That can only be one person. After piecing the pieces of puzzle together I'm certain, *it's Rhys.*

Her eyes catch mine then quickly dart away. Oh, don't worry little raven, so reserved and cold, you won't have to make the first move. I would be more than honored to bring a sparkle to your emerald eyes brimming with hatred and bitterness. To make your pink lips that form a thin line of grimness turn into a smile. For those woes are not directed at me, but everyone else who has ever troubled you.

She is cold and brash with words at times, I've heard. Yet is simultaneously one of the best socialites that had title. Like a beautiful flower; It only blooms when it has to, when it's time to. Never sooner. I can't help but wonder…why? What could possibly be her reason for the way she speaks in turn? Is it that her true colors slip out every so often from under her black veil? I guess I will have to find out myself.

I walk up to her and bow. "Forgive me your grace, I should have introduced myself sooner. I am Neclosse, from the country of Mardo. You may call me *Ari*, if you'd like."

Rhys 3

"I know who you are. You are the King's right hand. Or is it more formally—head monk or elder? My knowledge on Mardonian hierarchy and culture is a bit rusty."

"Abbot, if you want to be technical about it. But the duties run all the same." he smiles. "Honestly though, I'm a bit more flattered by the fact that the Queen of Minx knows me by name."

"I'm Royalty; I know everything, darling." I say.

Ari Neclosse, you are peculiar indeed. Your golden locks of hair, pale-green eyes, and nice build. You definitely have lived up to your reputation of being graciously forward for a monk. Not that I mind. We could use a few brave men in the world. Ones who enjoy a bit of a challenge, which I'm sure is how he views me. But watch out Ari, you don't want to bite off more than you can chew.

Nonetheless—I can't tell if you are truly bold enough to approach me, or truly that much of a fool. My name and status tend to run people off, even other Royals and nobles. He must know that.

Does he think he's immune? Because he was raised in the most polite country known to man? Or because he pretends to be humble? Is he confident, or just genuinely stupid? Either way, he's trouble. I can synchronously say he's attractive and no good for me. Ari is a man of games.

I am royalty, so I can lose everything at the snap of a finger. But him, he's no Royal. Plus, there's enough stigma in this world to convince any decent woman to avoid a man. We are shamed enough for sleeping with men out of wedlock—not that it has ever stopped me—he has nothing to lose, whether he acts impulsively or leads with his heart.

I can teach him a lesson. He's always the heartbreaker and never the broken-hearted, so maybe I will play along for now. But in the end, *I always win*. If he's willing to risk childishly wooing me, I have no problem watching him fall, *hard*.

Any other occasion, I would overlook someone like him. Many men, from afar and daringly close, have adorned me. But I tire quickly with simple-minded people. And I bore easily from a cat-and-mouse chase. This one might prove to be interesting and unique, though. I will enjoy toying with him; I've got nothing but time.

The entrance soldiers' horns blare throughout the center, echoing all the way to where we stand. My ears want to bleed from the incessant, unnecessary sound alone. *Ndam, sethe ppeole.* I attempt to block out the sound by covering my ears, to no avail. This means another Royal family has arrived—I wonder who it is?

"Introducing the King of Lynxsis, and his daughter, Lady Sandra." The guard announces as the doors swing open.

"Hello, fellow Royals." The King greets.

Oh, *it's them*. Never mind my initial curiosity, *please leave*. I hate people who flaunt their status. That's not unusual for someone in such a prestigious position; however, this particular Royal family thinks the world is their stage. Not to mention, I'm constantly compared to them and seen as a runner-up. It irks me and my country.

Simply put, the world is a better place without them. If they were to die in a fire or accident tomorrow, no one would care. I would graciously take their land, rule over their people, and everyone would live in peace. Yet, they continue to put us *through hell,* with every breath they take.

As they walk toward the incubator, the King—with such *wonderful* awareness—catches glimpse of the man to his right. "Aaugh—" the King gasps while clutching his chest, "who are you? Who allowed you in here?"

"Luke Merins sir, I'm a first-generation Magic user from Delnari."

The guard near Luke interrupts, "This is the boy who noticed the change in the artifacts. We deemed him worthy of being here amongst you. Shall we remove him?"

What Royal in their right mind gasps at the sight of his own subjects? There's no reason to remove him. He's a harmless person, so why the theatrics, Mr. Big Shot? Can't handle your loyal, kind subjects breathing the same air as you? I doubt you know what loyalty and kindness really are. Even if you did, you could never appreciate them; you're utterly arrogant and prideful. They really don't deserve their thrown, nor any position of power. One is supposed to use their platform to make a difference, not to seek gawking eyes of adoration.

"No, of course not, he could be of some help. Plus, we do not want to be rude, would we father?" Sandra responds to the guard, while giving her father an irritated look.

"Of course not." he replies.

Luke smirks as his cheeks turn pink when Sandra speaks up, coming to his rescue. Their eyes meet and quickly dart away. He steals another glance, not being able to help himself. Sandra's looking down at the tiled floor, to avoid more chances of eye contact. *She's so obvious.* I wonder if...

The guard breaks my train of thought.

"Gather around everyone," he instructs, "let's begin."

Luke 4

Oh, thank goodness, I'm safe. I surely thought that the King of Kings would have me thrown out at the blink of an eye—if it weren't for Lady Sandra speaking up. In truth, I should be thanking her.

I wouldn't expect any less from them, though. Despite treating and protecting a country well, the King isn't known to be friendly with his subjects nor others. I'm not directly under his rule, but his governing does affect me. It's because of the incident that occurred when I was a kid:

my family and I were forced to move to the trade-route area bordering Delnari and Lynxsis, near the farmer's market, where his influence is heavy. When I hear comparisons between him and Delnari's King, however, I sometimes wish I were on the other side of the border. Regardless, I wouldn't expect this one to host meet-and-greets through the streets of commoners in this lifetime.

His daughter seems more like the Queen; soft-spoken, yet speaks up when its deemed vital to them. Not known for many words, just powerful ones. At least I will be able to tell my findings straight to them. That way, it won't haunt me at night—wondering if it was relayed correctly to the rightful authorities. *If ever reported at all.*

"So are you going to prove your worth, or are you going to leave us here to stand and guess," the King states with disgust on his lips, "Luke Merins."

"Father…" Sandra warns.

Are they always like this? At each other's throats, making sure no lines are actually crossed. They've probably stopped arguments or potential war this way. If so, they need a subtler way of doing things.

I begin. "Right your majesty. So, I came by for my bi-weekly visit. I enjoy coming here to see the relics float amongst each other. As well as it's the most interesting thing for miles considering where I live."

"No one cares why you were here." Rhys interjects.

"But," I emphasize, "when I came mere hours ago, I saw the relics changing. The fire stone of amber started shaking—as if it were about to explode from some unseen cause of pressure. The water lily reverted back to a simple bud."

"That is not worth an emergency." says the King, undaunted at my words.

"What about the earth representative?" Rhys asks.

"The heart carved of wood looked to be rotting."

"Gross." exclaims the man they call Ari.

"The air feather lost hairs. The coin of illusion reheated, as if it were preparing to liquify."

"And the change of their rotation direction probably didn't help." Ari points out.

"But they look fine now." Sandra says.

We all look at our Relics. I stiffen up at the sight of the water lily regressing; it heightens my burden of introversion. Even more so, if this means I won't have magic. I feel like *hiding*. When I look around, Rhys just seems unnerved while she adjusts her cape. Ari tries not to look at them, worried of what he might see. Sandra stares at the gold coin to catch any hints of the signs I just mentioned.

For a split second though, they all changed. Everyone finally saw with their own eyes exactly what I had described. Even though we're suffering enough as is, we could only imagine the horrors of what's yet to come.

"Its occurrence is inconsistent." I add.

Rhys states, grimly, "This is worse than I thought."

Wow, even when she reluctantly wears worry on her face, she still manages to look beautiful. I want to smile at the thought of her beauty. But I don't want anyone catching me distracted. And I definitely shouldn't get side-tracked. I mean, these aren't just relics; they are the souls of our existence.

Especially mine. Not to be self-centered, because I have the least to lose compared to the others, but Water Magic is rare in my region. People like watching me perform Water Magic—I make friends with it by using it for good. Delnari needs me to have this Magic. *I'm worried.*

"It was a fluke I'm sure." the King is still not fazed.

The guard that once spoke for me, speaks up again, "Sir, have you tried using your Magic recently?"

"No, my daughter forbids its use for the day."

"It was my wedding day." she shrugs, her eyebrows lower.

The guard continues, "We've gotten some reports before your arrival. The Magic we use is starting to falter. Four people have come forward about this within a few hours. It'll only get worse."

"Where are these people now?" Ari asks, becoming more serious about the entire situation.

"Detained in another room, in case this was a ploy. We called you in to see if you had been affected by this turn of events as well, not just locally."

We all look at one another with hesitation filling our eyes. Nerves makes my body go numb. Even the King was unable to diminish how big a deal this information was. My palms start sweating profusely as my hands twitch.

Decisively, we attempt to use Magic at once. Some could conjure with their hands, others could emit from their entire body.

Nothing happens.

Not the tiniest hint of Magic flow. We all stood there— blinking, wide-eyed and jaws dropped. It's like we were broken, with no immediate fix. This means we're all *doomed*. There's no *Magic*; everything we do is based on *Magic*. We were like world-renowned performers who fell on their face mid-act, live in front of thousands of people. I feel defeated. Lost. Like I had more than Magic stolen from me, a piece of myself also gone. I close my hand in a fist.

Questions begin bubbling up in my mind. What would we do without Magic? What would happen when every commoner knew? They can't detain everyone. We rely on Magic, Royal or not. But the scariest thought isn't even that—it's the thought of never being able to fix it.

Sandra 5

"So really, what's our plan? We must do something—quickly." I rush them to reach a course of action.

The guards are looking to us, expressing that they're just commoners and have no idea. Truth is, we'll need all the brain-power we can get.

Rhys mumbles, "Well this is shitty. We definitely can't fix this problem overnight. This could honestly take weeks...months even. All Kingdoms will have to work on this together."

"What?!" I shout, losing my composure, "Absolutely not. My wedding has been interrupted due to these events. I spent time and effort preparing for this day, and you want me to just wait *months* so we can fix this?"

Rhys retorts almost instantly, "None of us asked for this to happen. As future Queen of one of the largest Kingdoms, you should know better than anyone. Royalty requires sacrifice."

"I don't need lessons in Royalty from you, of all people." I fire back at Rhys. *She's so smug.*

"Sandra." My father glares at me, warning not to step on any toes while we're here.

The guard, in hopes to change the current atmosphere, speaks up, "I would like to suggest you all take a journey east of here. You can go the abandoned forest in Lynxsis."

Ari interrupts, "Oh, so one of you *can* pitch ideas after all."

"Guard—you aren't talking about the forest of Oku, are you?" I wonder what he's getting at.

"Yes, I am. Lady Sandra, you must understand that no one is out there. No one will find you nor bother you. There's plenty of untouched land. Therefore, not only can you learn what's going on with Magic, uninterrupted, but if something were to occur, no bystander would get hurt by the mishaps."

"Guard, we can *die* in the forest you speak of—" I can't even finish my words before my father steps in.

"Daughter a word please. Outside. Now."

As usual, I straighten my posture, hold my head high, and try to leave the room gracefully. Though I may be composed on the outside, I'm shaking internally. My father pulling me aside always feels like a death-sentence waiting to happen. He is not only my father, but a King. Someone who can take my status away at any moment.

In our Kingdom, the crown-wearer doesn't have to be of nobility. You can be born into it, or you can challenge the current Ruler. It can easily be gained or lost at any time. For as long as I can remember, it's been passed down in our family, so no challenges have happened. Not yet, at least.

My father and I are outside, he's staring into the barren distance with a stern face as he waits for the doors to close behind us. Everyone around can sense the tension while they leave their posts to provide us with privacy. That's a good call on their part.

"Sandra, *what are you doing*? Do you care about your country at all?"

"*Of course* I do!" I'm shocked at that question.

"Well then, you need to embark on this trip immediately—no matter where it takes place."

"But—"

"If you do not go to figure this out, we will lose *everything*. Think about this logically; there is no other choice. Magic everywhere has been reset, for reasons unexplainable. The hierarchy as we know it, can change because of these events. If you do not figure out how to harness your abilities under these new conditions, there may not be a Kingdom to come back to. Of course, I will maintain order while you are away, but right now, everyone is equal. There's never been a greater opportunity to overthrow a Royal family. This trip is the only way to secure our reign. We will be able to see what our...*neighbors* are now capable of, as well."

"You're right." I exhale. I cannot dispute his points; he's a King, after all.

"Of course I am. I'm a King, after all."

Get out of my head, dad. "Well, we better get back inside and let them know of our participation."

"Good. Remember: this is your first act as a Queen." He reminds me.

"I know." I smile. Now I'm looking forward to the task.

We return inside to see the others mumbling among themselves. It's only now that I begin to realize it was a bad move speaking out of line earlier. I feel my heartbeat in my chest and thrumming my ears. "Apologies for my outburst, I am in favor of heading to Oku." I can't help but look down at the floor.

"So, apparently we need your vote," I hear Rhys say, "we were speaking about whether or not Luke—*the commoner*—should come along." I catch her shooting a snarky glance at my father while he's looking elsewhere.

"I think that'd be a great idea. Maybe he can provide an outsider's perspective. Show us how we can deal with our respective subjects, if we have to address the public regarding this problem when we return."

"Congrats Luke; looks like you get to spend time with glorious Royalty for an indefinite amount of time. What a *lucky* man you are." Rhys ends on a sarcastic note.

Luke lets out a nervous laugh when Ari pats him on the back.

"Alright then. Now that everything's settled, we all better be on our way. Not a moment to lose. You guards better hurry and get us a carriage and supplies." Ari continues.

The guards run off to make preparations. Not long after, we board our carriage and make our way to the forest of Oku.

Luke 6

Shortly after our carriage takes off, Ari suggests we all get to know each other better. No one really speaks up, though. Maybe it's because the girls and I were actually taking this trip seriously. Yet, this doesn't deter his relentless flirting with the girls, who don't seem to reciprocate his feelings. I envy his candor.

Man, if I could only borrow Ari's directness to express my feelings to my crush, while she sits in the same carriage as me. I'd comment on her beautiful eyes, her amazing heart, and how I admire the way she carries herself. I wonder if she'd even care; there's no chance of something happening between us. But, laying my feelings on the table may convince her to pick them up. I'm too much of a coward when it comes to women. Unlike Ari, who says whatever comes to mind—no matter how wrong it may be.

They've given him the cold shoulder since he started babbling, but Ari's persistent and patient. I'm sure one will give in. Hopefully it's not my crush; she's too smart for his games—I think.

"Come on guys, lighten up already." says Ari.

"Ari listen, if you don't want to take this trip seriously, fine. But I'm not here to make friends and play games. I'm here on business—to save my crown and protect my people." Rhys gives an extended stare after her words.

"As we all are. No need to spend every waking moment fretting over it, though. We have some free time. Loosen up!" he argues.

"He's not completely wrong." Sandra pops in.

Rhys isn't budged. "Business is always first."

"Is that for better or worse?" Ari isn't, either.

The carriage bustles and creaks as it runs over long vines and tiny pebbles. There's not much space to move around among us four, even with our supplies and food connected outside the carriage. We were just getting used to the minor bumps that jostled us, when we then rode over something large—sending us flying out our seats. However, that didn't stop them from jumping right back into their argument after quickly gathering ourselves. I could just barely hear the driver say his apology from the front.

I lost track of how long or short the trip was— entertained by their debates—but we arrive at our destination. You can see the sun peeking through the tall trees' dense leaves as we climb out our ride. The driver says he'll be back once he's heard from us, and wishes us well on our journey. He pulls off while Sandra, Ari and Rhys continue their talks of Royalty—and I'm intently listening.

We find a dirt path and decide to follow it. I notice Sandra's dress kicks up the dirt, getting it mucky. She's focused on her track.

"Aren't you hot in that heavy wedding dress?" Rhys says.

"Aren't you, in all those blue ruffles?" Sandra counters.

"I'd rather be hot and sweaty, than freezing cold."

When Rhys says that, my imagination has her and Sandra in revealing swimsuits, splashing in the water. I picture them drinking lemonade and applying sunscreen. Which is nearly opposite of this forest reality. We come up on an empty campsite of sorts. There might be a lake or river around here, though. Heck—I doubt they even packed something to wear for that occasion in their...

"Guys," I say.

"What is it, wallflower?" Ari adds one of his quips.

"Don't call him that!" Sandra outbursts, while placing her attention on me.

"Why not? For someone you don't know, you sure save him a lot—" I make sure to cut Ari off before anyone even registers his remark.

"Guys! Look around; we are in the middle of the forest with no supplies. *Zero.* And we have no way of calling the carriage back."

"Shit," Ari realizes our oversight, "I don't remember seeing the supplies behind the carriage when we stopped. We may have lost it in that giant bump on the road. Maybe we can walk back and get it."

"Yeah right. Who knows how far back that was. And how long it could take. We'd have to walk all the way out there on foot, *hoping* the supplies conveniently dropped, and walk all the way back. It'd be a waste of time." Rhys explains.

"Even if we did go back. I can't imagine it'll be sitting there in the middle of the road waiting for us. I mean we flew out of our seat when we hit that bump. Who's to say it didn't fling off into the bushes and damage all our stuff? Best case scenario is the driver sees our things on the road and returns to us."

Walking back sounds better than staying put, to me. "What are we gonna do, then?"

"Well, it sucks to be you guys." Rhys smugly replies. "In my country, survival skills are essential. So I can live off the land. And like I said: I'm not here to make friends."

"Is that your way of saying you won't help us?" Sandra asks.

Rhys smiles evilly in return, then disappears into the forest.

Of course she won't help us. A Royal could expand territory if another Royal dies, and she's already on

Sandra's turf. Easy to call dibs if no one else knows your rivals are dead yet. *Business first.*

"Uh, I'm willing to help, but I don't have the skills for this." Ari explains. I'm surprised he doesn't follow Rhys' suit.

I break three branches off a nearby tree. They're firm but flexible enough.

I hear a "what are you doing?" from Sandra.

I hand her and Ari a branch each. "I'm going to show you how to make a bow and arrow."

"Wallflower...*you surprise me.*"

While Rhys has abandoned us, I teach the others bow-crafting. We bend the branches and tie them with vines. It's only fifteen minutes before everyone has a makeshift bow. They're far from professional, but they can shoot a deer all the same.

"I feel better about our survival now. Thanks, Luke." Sandra says.

"Yeah, nice works Merins." Looks like I'm winning Ari over.

Moments later, we notice the gray clouds overhead have snuck up on us. They begin to thunder and crackle, causing Sandra to reluctantly wince.

"We need shelter, and soon."

"I know how to do that." I offer my services again.

"Me too."

Rhys comments as she reappears—from who knows where. No one asks either; we're too busy being pissed at her. We collectively head to gather leaves, rocks, and wood to pitch tents. *Drac vae lac.* At least there's one thing you can always depend on in the forest: wood, and lots of it. Trees fall all the time, so there's easy access. Rocks sturdy enough to stack, yet light enough to carry, surround the site. The trees are dressed with leaves larger than usual. All that's left to do is assemble the pieces with the twigs or planks of our choice.

Ari and I occasionally pass each other wooden pieces to save some trips between us. Sandra seems to spend more time on analyzing her choice of vines and rocks, rather than wood. I wonder if that's a Lynx thing; most of their buildings are made of stone.

We make hours fly as we complete our temporary living quarters. Across from me ends up being Rhys, to my left is Sandra, and Ari is my diagonal-left. In the center is a small pit we're using for a fire while we watch nightfall arrive.

Right before bed, I hear Sandra's murmurs in her sleep. I hope she's okay.

Ari 7

I'm awakened by Sandra singing. "Good morning everyone."

"Morning." we all greet back.

"I got up a little early to make these for you guys," she hands us grass-weaved baskets, "don't worry, it's weaved tight enough to hold water. I'm sure there's some nearby."

"How do you figure?" I question.

"It's an abandoned campsite, typically you'd set up camp near water, for easy access."

"Ah." *good point.*

"Well I'm off to hunt, see you later." Rhys calls as she departs into the wild.

"I'll go do the same, and keep an eye out for a riverbed." Luke follows up.

"What about you, Ari?" Sandra questions.

"Uh, I'll stay here and watch camp." I say, wearily.

She gives me a confused look but doesn't pry any further.

"You sure you'll be okay?"

"Totally." I respond with slight hesitation. She shrugs and leaves camp.

With that, I'm all alone with our constructed tents. I'm debating going back to bed. Judging by the sun's position, it's not even noon. I guess I'll get a fire started; the crackling from burning wood should be enough to break this lonely silence. I grab some nearby rigid twigs from the ground and crouch down to attempt making a spark.

That's when I spot him—A black bear with fuzzy fur, on all fours, roaming.

Oh no, *he's spotted me.* What do I do?

It takes a step in my direction. *No! Go away you six-hundred-pound fur demon!* It takes another step towards me and huffs.

I let out a shriek loud enough for all of Lynxsis to hear. A rustle comes from the bushes beside me. *Is it another one?* My feet are like concrete cinder blocks. My hands shake so violently that my nails dig into my skin after I clench them into a tight fist. Squeezing my eyes shut, I pray for it to go away. *Leave me alone. Just go*!

It lets out a roar; my eyes fly open to see the horror. It rises to its hind legs and looks at me viciously, baring its gnarly teeth at me. Raising its claws to attack.

Swoosh!

An arrow strikes it, right between the eyes. The bear freezes and its eyes gloss up like glass. Blood drips from its head. It falls backward and hits the ground with a thud.

"And that...is lunch." says Rhys, smiling ear-to-ear while lowering her bow.

Phew. I thought I was dead for a minute. But Rhys rescued me. I'm happy to be alive, though slightly embarrassed.

"You screamed like a six-year-old girl." she mocks.

"Shut up. I had everything under control."

"Oh, did you now? Then why don't you help me rip it apart, so we can have bear meat for lunch?"

"Are you crazy? I'm not getting anywhere near that thing."

"Why not?"

"It's probably diseased. What if it has rabies?"

"Well I wouldn't eat it if it was. Are you afraid?" she laughs.

Of course I am. My mother died from a seemingly harmless snow hare. My mom had taken it in, not knowing it had rabies. The symptoms weren't visible at first. Nonetheless, it scratched and bit at her, infecting and ultimately killing her. I was only five when she died.

Am I gonna tell Rhys that? *No way in hell.* I don't care what she'd say. That's a personal story that no one else needs to know.

"Whatever, kitten paws." Rhys rolls her eyes.

"Ha, kitten paws?"

"Yeah, cause you're about as strong as one."

"Oh, hush." Didn't know she could crack jokes.

"Doesn't matter, I must prepare our feast."

I plop down on the wide log across from her. She kneels by its head and rips out the canine teeth with her bare hands. Blood leaks through its mouth. *Not so tough now huh, bear?*

She slices a tooth into its chest, ripping it all the way down to the pelvis. She peels back the fur coat while slashing. Sandra walks up carrying her weaved basket.

"Nice kill, Rhys. Anyway, I found a river, thank goodness. Berries were nearby, so I put those in some water. A berry-infused drink is better than none."

"That'll be fine." I say, gliding my way over to her.

I put my finger to her chin, tilting her head up to me as I peer into her sparkling eyes. Her cheeks flush, a warm shade of red.

"I hope it wasn't too much of a burden."

She quickly turns away; her frizzy blonde curls slap me. She shoves the basket to my ribcage and walks past me.

Ouch. Did she just reject me?

I'm not sure if it's my pride or my body that's wounded. She hurt my feelings—*then again*—I still got her to blush. So, I guess I can call it even.

Ouch. Why is there a branch lodged in here? No wonder I felt like something was stabbing me. I pull the branch out the basket and toss it into the woods.

Luke returns about five minutes later. Sandra's somehow managed to manufacture a hollowed-out stone bucket for us to cook the meat in. She's proven quite handy. I've been munching on berries the entire time.

"No catch of the day from you, huh?" I ask.

"Well I admit, I didn't find anything. But I did come across a nice spot down the riverbed to bathe."

"Oh, that sounds lovely." a bloodied Rhys perks up.

"I brought back a bucket of water as well."

"Luke that's great." Sandra gives some encouragement.

"Great indeed. Now pour the water into Sandra's pail and let's start a fire, so we can boil us some bear meat." I guess the possibility of me eating rabid meat is less threatening than starving.

"Alright." Luke gets started right away.

We cook and stay warm while the temperature drops to a warm chill. Shortly after we dine, Luke and Rhys dispose of the carcass away from the camp.

It seems like things might be looking up after all; it's time for bed and we haven't killed each other.

"Goodnight kitten paws," Rhys hums as she heads to her tent.

I crack a sarcastic smile.

"What's that about?" Luke inquires.

"Let's just say...she learned something new about me."

"Like what?"

"My biggest fear." I mumble under my breath.

Sandra places her hand on my shoulder, "well maybe we can take your advice from earlier. We should all try something new: Face our fears."

"Heh, yeah." I smile back at her.

How did she hear me?

Luke 8

It's early dawn and the animals are active. I'm hunting for our latest meal; we devoured that bear meat in one night. There's plenty of rabbits, snakes, birds and such, but they wouldn't be enough to feed our group. After living with the everyone for three full days, I've learned a lot about our eating habits.

The bushes continue to rumble about; I try to remain low and quiet. It's been ages since I've hunted. After the King of Delnari moved my family and I from our home to further east, things have changed a lot. I went from a young boy learning to hunt and game for sport, to a caregiver of his now-elderly parents, who'd been farmers involuntarily. It's my fault, I admit it. But I also know it wasn't intentional.

I was being young and naïve. What was I *thinking*, roaming around the King's castle? It wasn't trouble, but that's surely what I found. The guards shouldn't have let me get that deep into the castle grounds to begin with.

King Robert the Third hosted a party, which entailed a giant banquet and a parade showcasing beautiful floats. It was for a matchmaking ceremony between our home country and Mardo. *If we only knew what we were actually celebrating.*

No...focus Luke. I must move on from my past. No excuses or justifications. But I cannot say what I learned that day, didn't change me as a person.

This forest is making me delusional. It's giving me too much time to think— overthink—about everything. I reminisce about the loves of my life...the way the world works...even time to contemplate on what I want to do with my life. I don't actually want to be a farm boy my entire life. Yet, I don't know what I'd do instead.

If I could I'd tell the world *how I love her*, I'd scream how no one has control of my destiny—if it's such a thing. I'd even whisper my dreams into existence. But I can't do any of those things.

There she is; so alluring and majestic. Innocently chewing on what she deems suitable for her needs. What a wonderful creature.

A deer, available for my hunt.

I prepare my bow and arrow without a sound. I stoop down onto my knees and peer over the bushes, keeping my eye on the target.

The glistening-brown deer continues to eat, unaware of my shot arrow making its way to her. A split-second before it hits, an innocent bunny hops into its line-of-sight. The arrow's graze slightly wounds it, but I still get the kill I came for. *Bullseye*! One shot kill! Maybe I'm not as rusty as I thought I'd be. Good to know.

I make my way over to the struggling bunny. Dammit, I'm sorry little guy. You're bleeding because of me and I don't like sending suffering animals back into the wild, especially when it was accidental. Why couldn't you hop elsewhere?

Its fur begins to stain and stiffen. The bunny twitches in agony. I wish I had something to numb your pain. Examining the wound, it may be more vital than I originally thought. You weren't what I was trying to kill.

I never liked death—even as a kid. Yes, everything dies eventually, it's a natural part of life. But it always feels like the innocent die the most. From the young age of four, death haunts me. I remember my cousin's funeral like it was yesterday. *Heart failure*, the doctor said. She apparently had a really small heart that couldn't support her body. All too young.

There she laid: in an oak box filled with dandelions at her funeral. I approached the casket with no expectations. I knew her body would be pale and motionless. What I didn't know, is that her eyes would be open. She glared at me, *taunting* me. Like her soul had left her body, and something evil was taking her place. The dread alone made me feel death's proximity. But I wasn't ready to leave my body. I'm not prepared for the tears of sorrow at my own funeral.

My biggest fear is death. I never want to see anything die. I never desired the innocent to die by my hand and suffer slowly in my arms. Yet, here I am—unable to look away and simply leave it for dead.

Abandon it, never look back.

I can't, it *needs* me.

I hold its paw gently and my heart fills with sorrow. I feel swirling inside my body. My fingers begin to tingle.

The hare begins to *heal...*

The wound slowly vanishes, and the blood is gone. No more stained fur. The hair even grows back. The bunny leaps from my arms and jumps around. Restored to full health—as if it had never been injured.

Healing Magic? Is that a thing? This is the first time any Magic has happened since it reset.

No, *this can't be.* Only five types of magic exist, *right?* But what else can I call it? It healed to perfection. I felt Magic run through my veins. More powerful than Water Magic ever did. It was purely me and my willpower. Wasn't it?

I can't dwell on this. I'm heading back to the campsite with the deer meat. I'll just keep this experience to myself.

Plus, what would I tell the others anyway—that I healed a rabbit with my *bare hands*? No way would they ever believe that.

Rhys 9

Another day at the special part of the lake I hold dear to me; I call it my *bath house*. It's a secluded area of the river. To my sides there are stacks of smooth, rounded rocks from the river. The branch leaves hang to provide shade, but allow just enough sunshine to shower through. The water hugs me at a temperature just below warm. I ripple the water to show my gratitude. This spot is the best part about this trip.

Even though the group hasn't been problematic, I still have my duties to fulfill. The stress from it sits on my shoulder. As my parents—who loved to remind me growing up—used to say: *I will always truly be married solely to my crown.* At the time, I didn't know how true it was and how far into my life it would pour into. But now I do...and I hate it.

As I soak in the water, my demons still haunt me. They whisper and call for me. Chanting that I follow my parents orders already. Like a robot or a puppet, I do what I'm told. Simply because it *needs* to be done.

Just like I *need* my crown.

Especially since it's not completely mine. I carry out a lot of Queen-like errands, but I'm nothing more than a face, for our people. I guess this imposter syndrome comes with the territory—which feels more than a little obvious. I never would've expected how isolated I would be though, and how distant I would become. In the end, it's all unfair. Everything in my life came from someone else's doing. And nothing I've had, has ever been completely mine.

Yes, I'm technically Queen, but it can still be revoked by prior Royalty, if they deem you unfit. That being said, maybe one shouldn't be crowned at the young age of ten, such as me. It's obviously a lot of pressure, but my family studies hard and learns survival-skills from birth. Mostly because we don't live long, but it's the least we can do. No one is immortal. Young or not, my parents gave me a tall order when I was 14. The order: kill Sandra at the most convenient time.

What would be more convenient than killing her in the Forest of Oku? If her death was reported from this location, I'm sure few would question foul play. We're in this hazardous forest with no Magic. Maybe her parents would, but they wouldn't be able to change the fact she's dead. Plus, Royals are pretty desensitized about death since it happens so often. That's just how it is.

I could kill Sandra immediately if I actually hated her. I could justify the order for a reason like closing a trade route we aren't even using, or interrupting an exchange between Minx and Mardo on Lynxsis territory. But she hasn't done any of those things. She's pretty nice, sadly. But her being nice doesn't change my orders—unless I'm willing to be disowned. And that isn't an option. I can't kill her based on existence alone, though. Just because she's Royal.

Yes, Royals are born to die, and yes, I often do questionable things. But that's my method of survival. Hence, I act cold, distant, duty-oriented, all while maintaining my Queen-like persona. This results in people hating me. So then, if I need to do something—like kill someone who hates me—I have no guilt. But Sandra seems incapable of true hatred. Which sucks, because her hate would make things easier.

There are other days as Queen that aren't as morbid, but still tedious. The days where I must be the perfect socialite adding witty commentary, solve a problem with apparent ease, and stay highly-attentive to an old man, droning on and on about his oh-so-exciting lumber trades. *My favorite.* All I get to do is represent my family by smiling and following orders. Always feared or loved, based on the given scenario. In the end, I just get the toughest jobs and none of the credit.

I begin washing my lengthy dark hair, taking out any leaves, twigs, or *bugs* that might've ended up in there from the last few days. Long hair is so much work. Maybe I can give this a good chop when I'm done here. *Yeah right*, like mother would approve of that. It'd probably look bad short, anyway. As I wash my hair, my self-pity slowly transitions into envy and hate. I stare off into the trees.

I *hate* how Sandra has everything come so easily for her. Or how the guys drool over her—though Ari probably drools over any girl he comes across. I hate her innocence and her very *existence*, because she makes mines so hard.

If it wasn't for her and her country, my country wouldn't always play second fiddle. My parents wouldn't have to pressure me into assassinating her. If she fell off the face of the earth, *I'd be free.*

It's settled: I hate everything about her. I will destroy everything she loves and touches. The way she took everything that is mine. Like the freedom I would have had over my own life. Where everything would be fine.

I notice this huge tree I've been staring at is now smoking. I then see a small flame burning at the trunk. As my body swirls with anger and fury, the fire grows larger, scorching through the trunk of the tree. I'm having intense flashbacks of my youth, displaying within the fire before me. I finally manage to snap out of it, grab my berry basket and fill it with water. I hop out the bath and dash to the tree. I douse the tree with the water, berries following suit. The fire extinguishes from one bucket trip, thankfully.

Those berries took me forever to collect. "Shit, I have to start over."

Sandra 10

Laying in a forest clearing, away from the others—actually feels quite nice. We spend so much *forced* time together, we all need a break. It's no wonder why we get unexpectedly angry with each other. But for now, I'm alone; away from everything, my only company being green leaves above me providing shade, and the sun peeking its way through. The wind serenades the area. It's beautiful and calming.

This is actually the first time since my so-called wedding I've had time to think. To miss my family. To reminisce about my brother, Ajani. He was so kind and sweet to me. He was nine and I was only six, when we last saw each other. He was my only friend and took good care of me back then. Even when my family had explained only one of us could have the crown. In most families, that is when they start to turn on each other and take on a selfish mentality, where some could easily leave their siblings for dead.

But Ajani and I weren't like that—we were closer than that. Even with our studies and parents treating us differently—yet fairly—due to gender, we'd always found ourselves being each other's better half. He covered for me if I broke something, despite my father's temper and discipline. Always stuck up for me, even if I was blatantly wrong.

The best part about Ajani was him being so talented in our Illusion Magic. He could easily change one's perspective of every room's appearance in the entire castle...*at once*. Maybe he could do even more, if he took time to practice. I never understood why; I just knew he was better than me. I knew back then, he was most likely to win the crown. But that wasn't worrisome in my eyes, because he loved me as much as I loved him. He wouldn't leave to fend for myself nor kick me away.

Ajani cared about everyone; animals, subjects, even orphans. He was very charitable and sociable. I wanted to be just like him.

Minus all the fighting he did with my father.

Ajani was also incessantly stubborn and outspoken. Whether it was the way my brother displayed Magic or refused to practice so heavily, it rubbed our dad the wrong way. My brother never liked violence, but father told him "a King must weaponize Magic, even if it's for his own protection alone."

Honestly, I was confused back then, *and I still am now.* How could the two men I loved more than anything, constantly *fight* all the time?

I roll over in the warm grass. Birds fly away at my subtle sound. I sigh at the wonderful memories.

They were a handful. Even when I asked Ajani to try getting along with father, they still would end up fighting. It's not that they hated each other, they just had a different outlook on the world; different strategies on reaching a common goal.

Then there was *that day*. I'll never forget. An April 23rd, my brother and father would get into their final fight.

They screamed and lamented.

Then there was silence.

My brother had been exiled. I asked my parents why, but they wouldn't give me a reason. They refused to talk about it. They left me in the dark about it and pretended he didn't exist, and treated me as their only child.

When I asked Ajani, he kind of talked his way around it. Something else he was good at. When I approached him, the only thing that really happened was the promise I made him. He had said to me that he was leaving, and I would be his little sister no matter what, and that I had to continue practicing my Magic and succeeding in my studies. He had me promise I'd never forget him. And so I promised him, I would never forget.

Not that I ever could, because I loved him more than anything. He was God's gift to man. Even though Klaud is close to perfect as one could get, he would never be my brother. Even at the altar, in this dress. Priest next to me, Bible in hand and our marriage almost solidified...deep down, I was still thinking about Ajani. I know in my heart that I'm Klaud's light at the end of his tunnel. Soulmate, I'm positive. *But Klaud isn't and never will be mine.*

I've tried convincing myself that I was in love. That maybe it was cold feet. That after everything was said and done, I could learn to truly love him. I was filled with second thoughts. I wanted to run away, but Klaud is a good guy. My father loved him. Most importantly, this is what Ajani would have wanted for me. To marry and take the crown and be the best Queen I could be. He always told me "the Queen is key in any puzzle, and the most powerful piece in chess."

Which is true for Lynxsis; the Queen has majority of the power, despite the way my father chooses to behave. My mom is Queen, but she is indifferent about nearly everything. Politics, animals, war. Almost to a fault. She just doesn't *care*. Maybe it's because she never took stock in power or money—she probably couldn't appreciate it fully, having never lived without it.

My father, though, he's always motivated and speaks with passion. The type of King people wish for and dream of being. He is a King at heart, down to the blood cell. Always with a sword in one hand and his passion in the other. Though it depends on who you ask, which one he actually uses more.

After all the heartache and tears about my brother's exile, I assumed it was because our dad just got sick of Ajani ignoring his direction. He simply didn't want to see Ajani, because Ajani refused to be the King my dad wanted him to be.

Truthfully, I didn't care what the reason itself was, I just want my brother back. There would never be a good enough reason for him to be sent away. I just hoped that if I did know, then I would be able to bring him back from exile myself. *Wherever he may be.* He could still be right here in Lynxsis, for all I know.

Sandra 11

A stir in the bushes catches my attention. I sit up and spin around to look in the direction the noise comes from. Oh, *it's just Luke*. I was worried for a second. Glad it wasn't a wild animal or something.

"Am I interrupting?" he says, as he stops in his tracks.

"No... I just suffer from a troubled mind."

"I'm all ears. A penny for your thoughts!" he says while approaching me again. "I'm curious what could be in that mind of yours. Especially someone of your status. Queen of the most powerful place on Earth."

"Many things trouble me. Are you prepared to hear my unfiltered flaws and sins, though?" I exclaim.

"If that's what it takes to ease your mind than yes." He sits in the grass across from me.

"Well, first you should know I am not an official Queen, as I am not yet married. I may be ruler, but one is not a true Queen without marriage. A prerequisite of my people. *A strong one*, I might add. We are people of tradition."

"And this troubles you? You were to marry a well-off man of nobility correct? Klaud, I believe?"

"Yes," I sigh, "but that's only because my title cannot truly give me everything I want. Especially when I know that in everyone else's eyes it's inappropriate—probably even crazy. It isn't suitable for someone like me."

"So, you don't...love Klaud?" Luke says with slight confusion.

"Not completely, not wholeheartedly—not the way I should." I stammer, "He is a good man, *really*. He is a strong-willed man and very motivated. He has his head screwed on straight—and gets along with my father."

"So, you don't love him." Luke states solidly this time.

"Of course I do love him...what makes you say otherwise?" I ask. I feel like I'm trying to convince him to convince myself.

"You've stated your troubles, yes. But you simply listed things you can find in any man that is fit to become a King. Nothing specific to him."

"Ah, so you have been in love then?"

He laughs, "Far from it. At least I think. I would call those feelings a crush, if anything. One that won't progress at all."

"What makes you say that? What makes you so pessimistic about love all of a sudden?" I inquire.

"She's far above my status, as I have none. She's beautiful and caring. I care for her deeply, but I'm not sure she knows I exist in the slightest. Not the way I'd like her to. Even if she did reciprocate my feelings, we could never marry in the people's eyes. It's a pipe dream."

"So you say." I follow up.

"I can't even talk to her without my heart about to jump out of my chest. I get tongue-tied and—it just never goes anywhere. Even if I've planned what I wanted to say."

I chuckle a bit in response. If I could only empathize with his pain. He struggles with speaking up. My problem is keeping quiet day in and day out. Similar, but on different ends of the spectrum when it comes to romance.

"I've made you laugh. Does that mean your mind is less troubled now?" He asks with a warming smile.

"Not completely," I say, "but if I tell you my sin, my greatest flaw and biggest secret, will you tell me yours?"

"Well it would only be fair." he tells me.

"My biggest sin. My truest love—is a man whose name is no longer mentioned. One that people dare not whisper. His name—Ajani Thorne. He was exiled."

"Ah...indeed...you have a troubled mind. You're in love with your brother, trying to make your heart love another." He's actually *understanding* my plight.

"See? I told you it was inappropriate. But I seem to be fond of you, Luke Merins. You seem trustworthy."

"Thank you. Now, I shall reveal my biggest secret—one I said I wouldn't share. But, a reveal for a reveal. I recently experienced my first bit of Magic."

"What?! you did?" I'm shocked. "Why haven't you mentioned it till now?"

Luke explains, "Well I wasn't completely sure, but I can't imagine it being anything else. It was unusual. I felt it pulsing through my veins. My fingers had a tingling sensation."

I interrogate further, "Is that all? What came of these sensations? What happened *before* these sensations?"

"Well the only other feeling I had was fear. I just wanted the bunny to be okay, not to die by my accidental arrow. Anyway, it healed. Its blood returned to its body. Hair that was grazed, came back immediately." he answers.

"That is...odd. But if you say it happened, then I believe you. It's the only clue we have to finding our Magic at all. But it's odd cause there is no Magic like that."

"I know..." he agrees.

I exhale a deep breath having shared my troubles with him. Though my secret was bigger than his, and I am still curious who is crush is, I won't pry at all. We both must deal with our own versions of issues. Albeit his magical experience is more helpful to the current issues at hand.

"Forgive me if this is asking too much, but will you tell me more about your brother Ajani? He must be interesting if he's captured your heart, despite being related and knowing how others will see you differently if you were to admit this."

"Gladly," I say.

I tell him about my brother and I as kids and some of the fond memories of him. His features I love. About Ajani's big heart. It was more than a relief to share everything with someone who actually would listen. Someone who wouldn't turn up their nose at the slightest mention of my brother's name. Luke listened to me, fully engaged until I had nothing left to say. I shared memories that I had nearly forgotten about. And Luke never questioned any of it or interrupted me in the slightest.

Luke 12

She's so happy and excited to be able to speak of her forbidden love. Even if it is her brother Ajani, who, in all fairness, does sound like a pretty good guy. With all of his perfection, I wonder if she could ever truly open her heart to another.

I understand how much she struggles with this. I know what it's like to not be able to speak about someone you care so deeply. Especially when they've helped you in your time of need. You can never seem to thank that person enough.

I know this type of love for her brother is wrong, but I can't help but think to myself: does he love her too? Or did they have a normal relationship when they were younger, and her perspective just went too far?

Not that I'm judging her or anything, because love is beautiful in all aspects. But I always believed love was not a conscious decision as much as it is something that just happens. Before you can even process it, your heart is thrumming joyfully in your chest.

And it might be selfish of me to even be thinking this right now. Sandra needs a shoulder to lean on, and all I can ponder is whether she could love me instead. A person who knows her biggest secret and yet still willing to wait. Should I really be thinking about a woman who is soon to be wed?

Then again, the fact that her wedding was interrupted and never finished because everything Magical, could be a sign from the gods it wasn't meant to be? What's the word? Mak ontree di Ah, divine intervention. Fate.

But what makes me an exception? Maybe it means she's meant to be with someone of status as usual. Just not specifically with her fiancé Klaud. Stop it already.

But I want to be with her—there is no hiding that. Even if she does love another. Yes, I am definitely being selfish. Well, at least I care enough to listen and keep her secret. She must trust me; anyone else would have taken this straight to the public or blackmailed her.

I can't complain, at least I have her attention. Which is something I craved. She's so innocent and understanding like myself. Not many girls like her nowadays.

My heartbeat slows at these thoughts. My head begins to ache from the frustration of trying to read the situation. It's all too much for me to handle. It might be only a fraction of what she's feeling, experiencing it firsthand.

How did I ever expect to be able to help, when I can't help myself? Did I mistakenly think her problems would be easier? Or did I think this would change my situation with her? Either one would be a foolish thought, no matter how I spin it. Well, it doesn't matter now. It inevitably seems like I'll remain stuck between a rock and a hard place.

Sandra continues to tell me about her brother and I just nod and listen. Attempting to not drown in my own thoughts and focus on what's really important: her feelings. If I don't pay attention and make her safe confiding in me, I won't be anything to her—and vice versa. That's not my goal.

Maybe I should ask for advice, considering how much of wallflower I am. I feel like I'm easily forgettable sometimes. I don't want her to forget me. Should I ask Ari for advice? He seems to be good with girls. Should I ask Rhys? She could give me a feminine perspective.

I swear, I never know when to quit. If all else fails, I'll just ask both. I mean, the worst that could honestly happen is nothing. Absolutely nothing. I'd never get out of the current state I'm in: indecisiveness and uncertainty. The last time I felt this way I was...

"Actually, Sandra, I need to tell you a secret." I say.

"Didn't we just do that?" she replies, confused.

"This isn't my personal secret though. This is a secret between countries. Between Delnari and Mardo to be exact." I explain.

"Why would you sell out your own King though? We were supposed to be exchanging our biggest secrets, yes, but are you sure you want to tell a Royal this? Although, being Royal, I might already know this secret. Either way, you've peaked my interest, therefore I'm inclined to listen."

Okay. "I was 11 years old and it was a big day for us. The King was hosting an open parade at the castle. Let's just say at the time I was higher up in the food change than now. Only slightly. Anyway, it doesn't matter. He was hosting all this for our most famous tradition: a marriage between people from one of either country."

"Yes, I've traveled to celebrate these proceedings on multiple occasions. I'm familiar with it." Sandra is listening intently.

"But did you know what you were really celebrating?" I ask.

"What are you implying?" she queries, leaning in closer.

"Well, I strayed from the crowds and floats to find a bathroom. I thought it was around a corner like I remembered, but I was mistaken. Nonetheless, I wandered around a few more corners until I had made one too many."

"Okay." she nods.

"Before I rounded the final corner, I heard voices. Specifically, the King and the Head Elder of Mardo speaking amongst each other. At first, I thought it was simple gratitude, but there was more to it than that."

Sandra's fully engaged now, waiting in anticipation.

I continue, "The King said that 'this was another match made in heaven.' The elder's response was 'yep, another well-made sacrifice of their souls after their honeymoon, I will get to live another 10 years of youth.'"

"Immortality..." she whispers.

"After that the King said 'such a shame their bodies must go rot in my sewers after.' The elder laughed, 'it's okay, all the money and resources I drown you in every wedding always seems makes up for it. You rinse your conscious with gold.' 'That, I do' my King said."

"How could you listen to these horrors?" she gasps.

"I was 11. I stood in shock. I was scared."

"But what was the motivation? Your King must've had some. What else does he get out of this deal? He's already rich and thriving. He's practically giving away his subjects to most likely Mardo's Water Spirits, if I recall their beliefs correctly." Sandra is perplexed.

"His secret."

"The only way to keep a Royal eating out of your hands. I wish I could say I was more shocked."

"The elder continued on to say 'plus, I keep your secret under lock and key. You not being Magical and all, on top of the reason for having no heirs.' 'Or family,' my king laughed, 'they were good for nothing anyway. Especially my brother.'"

"Wait a minute now. They really said all this? I mean honestly, why would they be bragging about this so loudly in a common hallway? They're Kings, after all."

"Exactly. They're Kings, they don't worry about getting caught. They can take off someone's head at their liking. Who's going to question them?"

"Fair enough, I guess." she hesitates.

"Listen, at first I didn't know what to think either. But later, after the occasion ended, the King asked my family to meet with him. So, my parents did. When they came out from the meeting, they didn't say much. But directly after, I was caught eavesdropping. After that summon, everything changed. Even then, I didn't know if what had been said was real."

"Especially with that immortality element." Sandra adds.

"My family and I were sent far east. We currently live near the border of your lovely place. A mere hour away from the Relic Center, give or take, hence why I was there so often. We were forced to become farmers and never saw our old friends again."

"That's not enough evidence though. Not in a country like yours."

"Well a few years later, my older sister Allie got engaged to a guy from Mardo. Wed before God, and sent off with an all-expenses-paid trip by the King. She never called, wrote, nor told us where she was. Almost like she fell off the face of the Earth. This was the same person who called home every other hour when she started college—a college only 3 hours away. She loved the concept of a tight-knit family, and that's what we were. She wouldn't change that...she couldn't if she tried."

"Alright, alright. I believe you." She tells me.

I sigh. "But there's nothing I can do."

"Maybe we could if we pulled ourselves out of our current rabbit hole."

We both sighed in unison and fell back onto the soft grass, bathing in an empty silence between us.

Ari 13

"Alright, it's a brand-new day. I'm going to face my fears today. I'm going to finally leave this camp and be useful." I recite out loud.

"Good for you, Ari. I believe in you." Sandra encourages.

"Whatever you say, kitten paws." Rhys inputs. "You said that yesterday, and you've made no progress."

"Who are you to judge how much progress I make?" I shoot back.

Rhys walks off into the forest with her bow and arrows. When I look over at Sandra, she gives me a gentle and hopeful smile, while fiddling with the basket in her hand. She awkwardly nods and wanders into the forest in the opposite direction of Rhys—I'm guessing that's not a coincidence.

I pack my weapons and basket. I'm on a hunt for a bear. I must find one and reclaim my masculinity. Then I won't have to worry about that terrible nickname kitten paws. I hear Rhys' voice echoing it in the back of my head. That's not the impression I want her to have of me.

The further away I get from the camp, the more I feel lost in the wilderness. I've already outdone myself by encountering some of the most disliked animals: worms, birds, ladybugs. All disgusting. But I haven't fainted yet, so all is well. However, my fear is not conquered till I deal with this bear. We'll save bunnies for another day.

I hear a huff behind me. The bushes swish while the wind stills.

Is this my opponent? I turn cautiously on my heels. The furry beast hasn't spotted me. A hairy black brute, eating berries.

Okay just walk up to it. Wait, who approaches a bear?

Conquer your fear, Ari, I say to myself.

I take a solid step forward. Major progress. It's still unaware of my presence. That's right bear...just keep eating. I'm a harmless human.

Taking another step forward, I break a branch accidentally, making a loud snap. Uh oh.

The bear looks over his shoulder at me. Eyes meeting mine, with no sign of wavering. My entire body shivers, contracts and undoes itself. I can't speak nor move. But— this isn't a panic attack. This is something different.

I blink, and when I open my eyes, all I see are leaves. Wait—no, this is grass. But how are they taller than me? The bear towers over me, sniffing.

I yell. All I hear is a tiny squeak. Oh no!
I look at my hands as I involuntarily twitch my nose. I begin to shake. I now have these tiny pink paws with nails. I stand up and attempt to look at my feet, but my new-found gray fur gives me away. I'm a damn mouse!

This is not what I signed up for. I wanted to be a man to face a bear; never thought I'd do it as a mouse. Great. I'm not even big enough to fight the thing. Had this happened any other time, I would've been overjoyed about being able to cast Magic again. But this was such a terrible time. Not to mention: I became something I hate.

The bear glares straight at me. I pretend to look around, taking advantage of my new form. I dash off into the taller grass until I think I'm hidden away. I'm going back to camp. Wait no, I can't—what if Rhys tries to cook me? What if they accidentally step on me? I can't talk to them. Not anyone. This fucking sucks.

Another realization comes to mind: I'm stuck like this forever. I don't even know how I got into mouse form, of all animals to become. How can I expect to change myself back?

Okay, think...I was afraid, and my insides were vibrating. So maybe if I re-enact what I did, I'll change back to normal. I take a deep breath and wave my little paws around. I close my eyes and focus...nothing. The bear seems to lose interest in me and wanders off, so I try a few more times. Nothing.

Maybe it'll wear off? How long will that take? Maybe if I dash around for a few hours, I'll tire myself and the Magic out. So, that's exactly what I do.

<u>Rhys 14</u>

I'm *sick* of all the back and forth. It'll all just go away if she mysteriously gets struck down in the forest. I mean, if this were to end now, and she were dead, we'd all part ways. Yes, her family would care she's deceased, but would they really minimize this Magic problem just because of a death? The reason we're out here is to keep it a secret and solve it as fast as possible. It wouldn't be worth it.

Plus, if everyone thinks its accidental, and I cover my tracks properly, no one should be the wiser. I won't be to blame and as long as that stands true, I won't feel guilty. Ok...even I don't believe what I just thought. *Why is this so hard for me?*

Alright. I don't need to justify my circumstances. I've made the decision to kill her. The next question is how. Can I poison her with something in the woods? Maybe a belladonna berry. Or should I just gut her like a fish? I could always bury her body, never to be found. I don't know, though, if the guys would let it go so lightly. They seem to rather like her. Well I'm sure I can convince them to let it go. We have lives we need to get back to.

Then again, Luke doesn't really have anything of high responsibility. He would have plenty of free time to dig all this up, if he wanted to. How nice it must be to have free time on your hands.

I worry too much, like always. So, I'll start simple and basic. I'll shoot her with my bow. Shouldn't be too hard to do without any witnesses. Everyone has a role to play in our survival out here, the boys will be busy.

Just to make it more fun though, maybe I can use this new Fire Magic I have, to make the kill.

A one-two combo. Step one: nail her with an arrow. Step two: set it ablaze, or make her explode into flames.

Who will know? As far as I notice, no one else has their Magic back yet. The others definitely seem like the type to share in such progress. Always about teamwork, with them. So, I'm sure they'll still be under the impression that I haven't made progress, either.

Little do they know that I have Fire Magic now. A power that I couldn't hate—nor fear—more. When I was a young Earth Practitioner, it made me feel weak. I was meant to protect nature and feed people with my Earth Magic, yet it burned it all down. Fire destroyed everything.

It was always cruel to me when I was younger. Minx had a terrible fire breakout. It was bad enough that we had to live in Tundra: a beautiful but vicious coating of white across all our land, with no blooming fruits. We imported those most of the time. We killed animals for our protein and forced our rare type of greens to sprout food of our choice. It was hard, because magically-sprouted food from the ground doesn't always taste natural or as good as it should. But we try our best.

Another time, this mysterious fire set aflame a commoner's barn, where many of our subjects received purebred animals for meat, donating to our communities for years. We were begged to come out and bring anything we could. Even if it was just fixing a section of the burnt barn.

So, the entire Royal family headed out after reports stating no one nearby could do anything, and we were their last hope. We were a family given such high praise for our beautifully strong Magic. *This was going to be a breeze,* we all thought. A simple snap of a finger and everyone would see our amazing skills. We couldn't have been more *wrong*.

We had arrived to the charred spot of where the barn had once stood. I was excited to help the people of our town, and to work with my family. We stood around in a circle, surrounding the dead terrain. Townsfolk watched us from every angle, hoping and praying to see it gracefully revived, replaced with flourishes of flowers and vines.

When we began the ritual, chanting and connecting our energy—Nothing happened. Nothing happened *at all* for the first fifteen minutes. We were so embarrassed. The ground remained in bad condition. It was like the fire was inside of us—breaking us down, not wanting to be healed. It felt *toxic* and resistant. I was the lead that day, but I couldn't do it alone. Something I had never encountered until that point. It was discouraging.

It's like in that moment, none of my talent or studious efforts made a difference. Like the life was being sucked out of me. Almost as if hell itself was messing with me, for shits and giggles. That day my self-esteem plummeted. Frankly, I don't know if I would say I have recovered since then. It still hurts like hell, and I should let it go—but I can't.

If I plan on mastering my craft and killing Sandra, I'm not left with much of a choice besides getting over it. If I don't embrace it and let go of my hatred, it'll only work against me. Even worse, I might accidentally harm everything around me. I might not be an Earth Practitioner anymore, but I still have respect for the forest.

So in the meantime, I'll just have a private target practice. I remember a nice sized clearing north from here. It's ideal for long-range shooting. I'll shoot there.

Ari 15

"There she is." I whisper to myself. "I spy...with my little eye...a raven on the hunt."

The raven, observant as usual, turns on her heels and points her weapons toward me, very determined to shoot. Rhys stands tall and strategic, glaring me down. Her right arm drawing the bow back, slightly shaking. She's angry with me for interrupting her session. Or maybe it's because she was hoping to hit someone else? I'm just glad it's not a mouse she sees.

"Will you put the bow down already?" I announce.

"Fine." she says, disarming herself.

"You looked quite lovely practicing. I know it's weird to say to someone who, mere seconds ago, was ready to strike me dead."

"Sure, yeah. I guess."

"What's wrong? You seem a tad distracted. Aside from me interrupting, that is."

"Nothing's wrong with me. Just target practice as usual? Why do you care?" she turns her back to me.

"Because it seems like your preparing to assassinate someone. But you're not exactly executing it well..." I trail off.

"What would you know about it? You can't even shoot a bear threatening your life." she points out.

"May I?" I say while picking up an apple she was likely keeping as a snack.

"Sure."

I prepare my bow and arrow accordingly. I toss the ripe red apple into the air as far as possible—probably a good ten feet. I aim then shoot it mid-air at its peak, splitting it in two with my arrow. Rhys catches them both, one in each hand.

"I *never* said I couldn't shoot."

Rhys looks more annoyed than impressed. "If you could shoot, why didn't you? The point of having the tools to begin with is to kill, hunt, and protect yourself. If not that, then what's the point of learning?"

"Maybe for most," I began, with a slight smirk, "but I had other motives for learning. None of which you listed, but a reason nonetheless. One that doesn't involve pesky animals."

"Really. What could it have possibly been?"

"Well for most it's a skill. Myself, on the other hand, I prefer to see it as a talent I can use to woo women. Tell me, is it working yet?"

"Nope, not yet." She snickers at me in disbelief.

"Damn it!" I laugh under my breath.

"You're such an idiot." she states.

"An idiot smart enough to know you're planning to kill someone. I'm guessing it's someone we know—as it seems like you're impatient. You're shooting at point blank range—as if you know you can get close to them. Not to mention the look you gave me when you saw who was standing behind you. Disappointed. Wanting me to be someone else, perhaps?"

"So what? Those are common sense. It doesn't prove anything." she says as she starts firing arrows at a tree that already has enough bruises. You'd think it was a woodpecker living there.

"You hesitated." I say firmly.

"And?"

"You've never killed anyone before, have you?"

"Of course I—" she exhales, "why are you doing this to me, Ari?"

"Why are you lying to me?"

"Answer my question." she demands.

"Simple. You plan to kill someone. You don't know what you're about to get yourself into. You're going to have someone's blood on your hands. It's not the same thing as hunting. Killing a person will haunt you forever. It doesn't just go away. You don't forget it."

"You don't think I know?" Rhys says becoming defensive.

"You're not gonna be able to kill her with a makeshift arrow, you know."

"I never said who it was." she says, surprised and thrown off. She glances over her shoulder and peeks at me.

"Rhys, I think you've made it pretty clear you hate Sandra more than anybody. What we don't know, is *why* you hate Sandra so much."

"Trust me, everyone hates her. They just don't want to admit it."

Rhys turns away, not wanting to acknowledge my presence any longer. Now she's trying to hate me for calling her out on it. But the facts are the facts.

I walk over to her and stand directly in front of her. As I look down at her, she stares at her feet, avoiding eye contact. I place my hands on each of her arms.

"Or maybe the truth is—you actually like her. And it's really *you* who refuses to admit it."

She shoves my hands away and breaks away from me. Is she feeling embarrassed? Vulnerable even? *The famous Rhys Crow.*

"Go away..." she whispers.

"Hey," I state, "look at me."

"Screw you."

"I'm serious."

She looks up at me, eyes watering. She's resisting her own feelings. Trying to hang on and hide the pain. I feel as if this is the first time she has really ever cried. This would indeed be the place to do it. Where no one could see nor judge.

I take my thumb and wipe away her freshly formed tears. I pull her close to me, my arms wrapped around her. She buries her face in my chest and begins weeping. I stroke her soft jet-black hair gently.

"It's okay. You know what—I'll do it for you. You don't even have to worry about it, alright?"

My heart thumps in my chest. My stomach is light. And I feel warm inside. Not at the thought of the deed I just signed up for. But because I'm *holding Rhys close,* doing the deed for *her.*

Rhys 16

"You know what?" I whimper uncontrollably, "I think I'm done for the day. We should head back."

"Okay."

Ari and I make our way back to camp, his arm around my waist the entire time. When we arrive, the others seem to be out and about in the forest. Despite the night sky beginning to cover us.

"Well, goodnight." Ari says, heading towards his tent, as I open the entrance to mine.

"Uhm...Ari," I hesitate barely above a whisper "You can come in, if you want. I mean—I don't mind."

He tilts his head to the side, wondering if he should take me up on this offer out of the blue. Almost as if it were a trick question of some sort.

"Please?"

"Alright."

He comes over to my tent and we both head inside. He lays down on the left side and I immediately on his right. We're so close, yet Ari doesn't seem to mind. Almost as if this were completely natural. Which it isn't, as the tent was meant for me only.

"I assume you wanted to talk more?" he asks.

"Well...I did. I have a question for you." I respond.

"Go ahead." he urges me.

"Well. I'm mean, cold, and nasty. I bully others and give everyone a hard time—for many reasons I won't list. However, you still want to put that aside and help me. Why?"

"I seem to grow fond of your distant ways. Being alone all the time. Always being strong, even when no one is watching."

"But Ari, we aren't talking about that. I mean...you volunteered..." I lower my voice to a mumble, "to murder a person."

"Yeah I know."

"Aren't you scared? I mean, you shouldn't be doing this for me. It's a bit much."

"You're right. Too much for you to handle. So, I'm filling in for you."

"Ari—"

He cuts me off, "Listen, there's no reason both of us should be cold-blooded killers. I already have blood on my hands."

I shoot him a look of confusion with a raised eyebrow. What did he mean by that? Was he implying the obvious?

"Promise to tell no one." looks like I'm going to get my answer.

I nod in agreement. Was I finally going to learn something under the surface of the man called Ari

Neclosse? First crying, and now this. That's two miracles in one day. Something's in the air.

"As far as everyone is concerned, I'm the right-hand-man of The Elder of Mardo. Like you said when I met you, everyone's heard of me. What they don't know, is that I was sleeping with his wife—without his knowledge, of course. We never meant for it to happen. But it did. We thought about the way things would end if he ever found out, that it would be better if she and I—"

I grabbed his shirt and pulled Ari in, kissing him. His lips soft and nice. Our warm bodies touching. Instinctually, he places his hand on my hips and pulls me closer.

He then pulls away and shakes his head as he sits up. "This isn't right. I feel like I'm taking advantage of you. I mean, your head's not clear. And with everything we've talked about. We're—"

"Closer." I smile as I sit up and look at him on eye level.

"Yes, of course—I mean, obviously." he stammers.

"You're attracted to me, aren't you?"

"Of course, Rhys."

"So then, what's the problem? I mean we both want this. For some time now." I place his hand back on my hip but he lets it slip off. "That's it then? Don't fight it." I whisper.

Ari moves his hands to caress my face. "Are you sure you want to do this? With me?" he questions, staring into my eyes. His face centimeters away from mine.

"Yes."

He kisses me with more emotion this time. With more passion from his heart. Not the façade we share. But our actual hearts. Though, I'm sure by morning our hearts won't exist at all.

Ari lifts me on to his lap. His kisses are sweet like licorice. I begin to feel warm all over. My heart beats wildly and nothing else exists. He doesn't just kiss my lips. He kisses my shoulder and the crevice of my neck—which slightly tickles. All while undressing me.

In turn, I undress him, revealing his amazing body. His skin is smooth, his abs perfectly toned, his arms strong. My face turns red.

"Like what you see?" he smirks.

I glance away from him. His body is so perfect. I never would've expected this. I can't bear to admit it. I bite my lip lightly.

"So, you do like what you see." he says in a teasing manner as he crawls on top of me.

He plays with my hair and drapes it like curtains over my shoulders and breasts. I wrap my arms around his neck.

And that's when he invites himself in.

Sandra 17

"Oh, you're up late," I say, spotting Ari on a log outside his tent.

"Yeah, Usually I would be sound asleep, but I felt like it would be a good night to go on an after-hours walk and look up at the stars. You know, put this whole situation behind me."

"So basically, you're stressed." I say. "Well you're not alone there. I've felt lonely for a while now, too. The only companion is the burden we carry."

"I guess that just makes us a pair of troubled minds then." He replies while staring at the dirt between his feet.

"Long as we remember that we have each other to share the burdens with, it should be easier. I mean we're all stuck here for the same reason." I say, smiling. "There's you, me, Luke, Rhys..." I trail off.

"What about you?"

"What about me?" I question.

"What if I just want to share my burdens with you?"

"Sure, I mean—I guess that's okay."

He smiles.

We both just stare into the fire and watch the freshly-chopped wood burn. The golden-amber flecks wandering off. It might not be the best scenario, but moments like this are still appreciated. The sounds of nature; the world's original—and very loud—lullaby. It's not always stressful. At least I pretend it's not.

"You know I've been feeling really homesick lately. Which feels weird because we're still in Lynxsis. Yet I feel so far away. I can't imagine what it's like for you and the others."

"I think it's about the same. Missing your family is all the same, the distance doesn't change that."

"I suppose you're right."

"Do you ever think," Ari begins, "about how the world around us is so dazzling? We never truly take time to appreciate it."

"It really is. We take Mother Nature for granted. So, I try to treat her well."

"You know, there's something even more beautiful than Mother Nature. I've seen it with my own eyes."

"Oh really, what is it?" I look at him filled with curiosity.

"You." He says smoothly.

My face flushes with color. I blush uncontrollably and look away. Does he really mean that? I can't believe he just gave me a compliment like that. I shouldn't be feeling this way over a silly pick-up line. It means nothing.

"Too much?" he follows up.

"Um, no no. It's fine. Uhm, I—I'm engaged and so, you know—" I stammer ridiculously; I'm an idiot.

"Oh I'm sorry, I didn't mean to offend you or your marriage or anything," he apologizes.

"It's fine. You know what—I think I'm gonna head in." I say as I stand up, preparing to leave.

"Please don't." he says. "Stay. I'll go. You came out here to enjoy the peace and quiet. I've been out here far too long as is. Plus, I'm the one who crossed the line."

Ari looks down at me into my eyes. I can see the reflection of myself and the flames in them. His eyes are gorgeous. They're *captivating*. I could spend an entire night looking for myself in these. My heartbeats feel louder. What am I doing? *When did he get so close?*

"So, I'll go then." Ari whispers.

I bite my lip and nod.

Ari starts to walk away. I almost let him. But then words fall out my mouth unexpectedly. My heart still thrumming.

"Ari," I call to catch his attention, "remember when you were saying, on the beginning of the trip, that it didn't all have to be about business? How we could just have some of the time to ourselves?"

"Yeah…" he agrees, vaguely recalling the memory.

"I was hoping to try something different. But I don't really know how."

"Have you ever been to the lake at night?" Ari interjects.

"No."

"Well I guess we should start with a late-night swim."

From there, Ari and I walk to the lake. There weren't many words exchanged on the way. The moonlight sparkled on the water. It was absolutely *astonishing*. The tree leaves fell slowly into the water, making ripples. I wish I could stay here forever.

Ari grabs my hand and leads us towards an overcasting cliff. We end up walking up the side of it. And when we arrive to the top, he stops.

"Watch closely." he says to me, "But first—" he plucks the veil off my head and places it to the side.

He runs and jumps off the cliff side's edge. I run up toward his launch point and look down, moving the hair out of my face. He resurfaces shaking the water out of his hair and looks up at me.

"Are you crazy?!" I shout.

"Maybe!" he yells.

"Isn't the water cold?"

"Come and find out!"

"But I'll ruin my dress."

"You said you wanted to do something crazy; here's your chance!"

My heart sinks to my stomach at the thought of jumping. But even as a kid I loved swimming. Ari was comfortable jumping in, so it can't be too cold if he's still in there. I guess I'll take my chances. I back up and run towards to cliff and jump.

I fall through the air feeling weightless. I don't worry about the water, my problems, my family. All there is, is me, Ari, and nature surrounding us. I plunge into warm water and that hugs me with a cozy embrace. My heart finally at peace, beating at a normal tempo. I emerge from underwater.

"That wasn't so bad now, was it?"

"Not at all."

Ari splashes me with water, "Good!"

"Hey! no splashing." I protest with a splash.

"Why, you afraid to have fun?" he says, shoving water at me continuously.

"No way."

"Then catch me if you can!"

Ari swims away and I follow trying to catch up. I enjoy swimming and racing after him. This is probably the craziest thing I've ever done in my life. In turn, it's the most fun thing I've done too. Just able to relax and be free. Soaking in this moonlit night.

I finally catch up to Ari.

We both stand the water, it being shallower in this area. Surrounded by smoothened rock and jungle. I brush water out of my face and look up at Ari. I grab his arm.

"Caught you."

"Yep."

We're standing close again. But my heart is fluttering. What's with this feeling? He leans in closer. I can feel his pink lips practically on mine.

I shouldn't want this, *but I do*. Despite this being incredibly wrong, it feels ironically natural. Like I can release control; something which I tend to not have any say in. Having self-control all the time is hard. In this situation, I'm not sure I even have it.

"We shouldn't." I whisper, "I'm practically married." as he caresses my face with hands.

"That's what makes it an adventure."

Ari kisses me and I light up inside like the glimmering moon. It feels like a calm ripple in the water. Like sweet honey. I don't hesitate to kiss Ari back. Nor do I think about how this could change things for me. Having to keep this a secret. *Maybe secrets are a good thing.*

My back gently touches the rock behind me. Ari pushing up against me. This is more than adrenaline. I'm overflowed with pure ecstasy.

"Do you want to continue with this?" he whispers while kissing my neck. "You're practically married."

"That's what makes it an adventure."

Ari 18

She is so delicate and innocent, I'm surprised this night is happening at all. To land a girl like her is really something. I know I make a lot of mistakes and sleep with many women, but that doesn't mean I don't appreciate them and everything they do.

Kissing Sandra makes me feel like I'm a different person. Like, I'm not Ari: the guy with a bad reputation. But just Ari; a normal guy. No title. I'm only human and we're a small piece of the universe. I feel vigorous and invincible. Like the world is on my side.

My body begins to vibrate. *Not this again.* Am I the only one who can feel this vibration? I break away from Sandra; the moment is lost. She's shocked. I look at her with worry then run off, splashing and fighting the water with haste.

"What's wrong?" she questions.

But I don't have time to answer. She can't see me like this. I make my way out of the water—never looking back at her. I don't want to see her reaction. I'm hoping she doesn't think I'm rejecting her or regretting.

"*Ari!*" she yells.

That doesn't sound like disappointment. More like *pure anger.* Hell hath no fury like a woman scorned. I hear her splashing through the water towards me. I reach the shore and run into the trees and peel off my remaining clothes. I leap over a few tree roots and feel myself transform midair.

What am I this time? I shake the dripping water off my fur. Wait, *fur?* I see my paw prints as I stomp in the dirt. I sit on my hind legs and brush my hair back. Is that a *mane?* I'm a lion now.

Note to self: don't roar at Sandra.

I stand on all fours and race to where I left her, hoping she's still there. Did I ruin things with her in the long run? Does she hate me? Running to her feels like an eternity, but when I finally do, she looks taken aback. Standing at the shore, her feet in the water. She seems scared.

The moonlight still beaming on us, now with a different set of emotions. Will this night be salvageable? Or will she want to forget it all together? I've never been this unsure before. There's no way she will understand everything that just happened. Hell, I don't.

She looks at me with eyes hinted in fear. How can I make her understand it's me? To not be afraid?

I stick my tongue out at her—feels a lot different as a lion.

"Ari, is that you?"

I walk up to her and rub my mane against her. She relaxes a bit. I can't talk to her so this will have to do. She pets me and looks down.

"So, it is you? How long will you be like this?"

I look up at her, not sure how to answer in my current form. Am I supposed to use morse code or something?

"Oh, right. Sorry. Do you even know? Make one splash for yes, two splashes for no."

I splash twice.

"So, you don't know, aye? I'm sure it'll wear off soon. I wonder how you felt when you changed into this. If so, you could maybe do the opposite? I don't know."

I let out a small growl.

"I have an idea. Wait here, okay?"

I splash once lazily in the lake. She better not abandon me out here. She runs her hand through my mane. Sandra takes off and disappears like I had done. Is this how she felt? Is this how I make women feel? After a few minutes, she returns.

I howl a hello.

"Ari, don't hate me—but I'm pretty sure this is gonna work."

She tosses something on me, landing on my back. I feel it start wiggling in my fur. Oh my God—*it's a bug*! It's trying to get me! I start rolling in the water uncontrollably. She threw a fucking *bug* on me.

"Ari! Ari! You're human again."

I stand up. *She's right.* I still can't believe she threw a bug on me. She tried to *kill me.*

"Oh, and I found these." she throws my clothes toward me and I dress myself.

"Better?" she asks.

I run up to her and pick her up and spin her around. She squeals with happiness. I put her down to a light sploosh.

"How'd you come up with that idea?"

"Well, it's just that—I figured if you panicked and let go of control a bit, you'd wear out your Magic."

"Thank you."

"No, thank you." she says, "Tonight was the first night I've ever had fun. Not to mention, this is the only day since the incident that I've felt Magic flow in my body again."

I give her a look. *Are you sure it was only Magic?*

"I know what my Magic feels like. That was it. Trust me."

"I do trust you, just glad I could assist." I respond. "Well it's beyond late. I think it's time for our *secret* adventure to end."

"Agreed." she answers as we begin walking to the camp.

<u>*Sandra 19*</u>

Before I left camp this morning, I saw Rhys and Ari arguing. I would ask what it's about, but I thought it'd be wiser to not ask someone that hates me. Luke seemed to be okay. I wonder how he's doing? I haven't spoken to him since we've last shared our secrets.

I cast the numerous worries aside; this moment is supposed to be about me. The sun beaming on my back. Wearing this leaf-woven tube top and grass skirt has proven to be more uncomfortable than I expected. Better than nudity though. Today is a day I share with *my* thoughts.

I hold my wedding dress in both my hands to take a look. It's so marvelous. I drop it in the dirt and step on it, flipping it over, making sure it gets everywhere on the dress. I bend down and lay it out, so I can see it well.

I start tearing the dress from the bottom to the upper thigh area. *Don't want to tear it too much.* This should make it easier to walk in.

I change my mind. I step on the dress and tear off the train. Ripping the dress from a beautiful floor-length fashion statement, to a cinch pouf dress with slits.

"This wouldn't have anything to do with me, I hope." A voice calls.

"Huh?" I spin around, spotting Ari. "Uh, no. You're not that important, sorry."

"*Ouch.*" he replies sarcastically.

I continue tossing it around in the dirt aimlessly. Occasionally shaking it out to see which parts have stained.

"Then why ruin such a beautiful dress?"

"It's not ruined. It's changed, *like me*. We've been in this forest a while now. I've finally had to survive and make decisions for myself. Yeah, I've helped out and encouraged teamwork before. But I never cared about what anyone else thought about me, not even Rhys. I'm always so obsessed with my image, Ari. It *consumed* me. Not anymore. Being in this forest has made me realize that, at the end of the day, my image is not going to save me. It's my actions, that will."

"It's symbolic." he whispers.

"I'm transforming into a different person. To a better version of myself. An actual individual, not just what people expect of me."

"Spoken like an honorable Queen."

I laugh at his remark. What is *honorable* anymore? I think everyone is corrupt, one way or another. So, I'm not sure anyone knows what honorable means anymore. Or if the word has just lost all weight.

"I'm sorry, I was rambling." I say, getting up. "Um, did you need something? Were you looking for me?"

"Yeah—right. So—I know we agreed to not tell anyone about our adventure. But I just wanted to make sure we were on the same page."

I give him a confused look. "About?"

"Well, the *obvious*. But I was also hoping the Magic would stay a secret as well. Because, well, I'm not ready to share that with everyone else yet. I don't have a handle on it, and—"

"I understand," I say, cutting him off. "I won't tell anyone."

"Again; very honorable. Anyway, thanks. Oh—and watch out for Rhys; she's already suspicious." He says as he walks away.

Back to *changing* my dress. I admit: I like it better this way. It's more camouflage, embracing the Earth. I was sticking out like a sore thumb. No more tasks nor doing what I'm told. I'm embracing my inner warrior.

I shake the dirt off the dress as much as possible. I hold it before me in both hands again and walk with it into the lake nearby, until the water is up to my waist.

"*Come closer.*" I hear a voice whisper.

Not able to identify a direction, I just ignore it. I start rinsing the dirt out of the dress, violently rubbing the fabric together. Was hand washing clothing always this *tedious*? Then again, I did stain it on purpose. Well at least I getting the look I was going for. I wring the water out and repeat the process.

"*Come closer to me.*" the same voice whispers. It came from ahead of me, this time.

I walk further into the lake until the water is past my bust. It's kind of hard not to be nervous, with the water being so high. I turn to head back.

The water around me abruptly starts to swirl. I look back. It swirls into a *figure of a woman*.

What is this? What's happening? Should I swim back or wait for the unknown?

"Please—do not be afraid," she states, "I am a Water Spirit; I mean you no harm. I have come to give you a gift."

"What gift?" I say, bewildered.

"Your Magic, of course."

"A Water Spirit's going to give me Illusion Magic? Okay, yeah—I've apparently lost my mind."

"A new era of Magic is upon us. The system has completely changed. It is to better humanity. To build stronger people."

"So I'm not going to have Illusion Magic anymore?" I question.

"In this new world, people must face their fears and surpass them. Embrace them."

"So it definitely wouldn't be my former Magic. Everyone's Magic would be different from what they once had. Some won't have any, because we don't all know what our true fears are."

"Don't worry, sweet child. Everyone will be graced with it, one day. Today you will receive yours."

"What is it?" I ask again.

The Spirit leans in and the water swirls once more. She extends her right hand towards me, graciously placing her pointer finger on my head and whispers.

"*Corruption.*"

Rhys 20

"So, you slept with her?" I ask bluntly.

"Does it matter? Are you jealous?" he smirks. "What do you care anyway?"

"Because you promised you'd kill her, not sleep with her." I whispered.

"So now you're telling me how to do my job of killing someone, despite having never done so yourself. Interesting." he says with no emotion.

"You're not taking this seriously at all, are you?" I question.

"Trust me, I am. Just have some peace of mind in not having to do it yourself."

"I won't have peace of mind until the deed is done. Plus, how can I be calm when you're compromising your position?"

He laughs, "*Compromising my position?* Wow, you really *are* jealous." he says as he gathers his weapons for a day of hunting. *More like escaping this conversation.*

"Ari, this is serious."

"As you've said. And I'm not compromising my position."

"Then you didn't sleep with her?" I say, glaring at him.

"Didn't say that either."

"Then you're compromising your position!" I yell at him.

"Okay, *mom.* I'm sorry, *mom.*" He mocks.

"What'd you say?"

"I said you're paranoid. Yes, I slept with her. Not that it's any of your business." he says, brushing me off. "You know, honestly—I expected Sandra to be the one to get emotional over me. But it looks like you're the annoying one."

"I am not." I protest.

"So you're saying it meant nothing to you? That there were no emotional strings attached?"

"Of course not."

"Then why are you still standing here with me?" he queries with a smile.

"Listen. If you don't kill her, then I will."

"Now you're changing the topic to not answer my question. Bravo."

He leaves the camp and I'm now here alone. Aggravated with the whole situation. I mean, I don't know what to expect anymore, honestly. Everything is a blur to me. I'm not sure where the line is anymore, nor if and when it was crossed.

I don't need Ari anyway. He probably won't do it, in the long run. So I guess I should pick up where I left off. I don't need any more target practice, but I do still need Sandra to hate me. It'd make it easier for me to kill her, in my eyes. But how could I do that?

Luke comes back from his hunt with dead rabbits in his hand, hanging by their white fluffy ears. *I should throw one on Ari.* Oh, the satisfaction I would get from watching him *squirm.*

Luke likes Sandra a lot. Maybe I can use him as a pawn, of sorts. Sandra would hate for something to happen to someone so innocent. Especially him. Based on the looks they gave each other that day in the Relic Center, I'd say he's the perfect target. At this point, he's all I have to work with.

"Hey Luke...back from your hunting trip, I see. Don't you ever get tired? You do it all the time." I say as I walk over to him.

"Well, we do have to eat. So it's not like we have a choice. Not to mention...day one, you said you weren't helping. So, yeah."

"Don't hold it against me."

"Heh. Um—how are you, I suppose?"

Wow he's making this really hard for me. He's so *awkward*. I'm not sure what to say in a subtle-enough way without being too forward or anything. But he's so—I don't know. Upright. Never dealt with a guy like him before, truthfully.

"Fine, I guess. Was wondering if you wanted to take a break with me? I could really use the company."

He contemplates the words I just said. *Can he see right through me?* Quick, say something *dummy*. He's your last chance after all.

"We uh—could just sit and hang out in my tent and talk about our lives. I mean, we haven't really talked much since being on this trip."

"That's because you don't like me!" he laughs.

Wow, harsh much. I mean I know I'm cold, but I expected more obliviousness from him. He's the nice one after all. What's his grudge against me? Oh, right—he likes Sandra and I don't.

"Will you give me a second chance? I want to get to know you."

"Fine, sure. I mean why not; there's nothing better to do out here anyway. I can deal with the rabbit meat later. Wouldn't kill me to socialize a bit."

"Yes." I squeal.

We head over by my tent and sit. Great.

Now what do I say? When did talking become so hard? Then again—my family are the only people I talk to, and I hate talking to them.

"So, what do you like to do, when not being stuck in a forest?" he asks me.

"What do I like to do?" I repeat.

"Yeah, do you like art, sports, baking?" he suggests.

"I—don't know. No one has ever asked me that before. I'm a Royal, so I don't really have time for things like that."

"You must have *some* free time on your hands."

"Nope, this is a first."

"Well then, being Royal sucks." he jokes.

I laugh in return. "Agreed, it does. But what about you? You must have plenty of free time on your hands."

"Well I live on a farm, so now it's just a lot of work. But when I was a bit younger, I used to entertain the other children with my outstanding Water Magic skills."

"Oh, did you, like, make water sculptures or something?"

"Nah, I used to juggle water, or do water park-like tricks. A lot of bubbles that they'd poke at."

"That sounds—"

"Boring? I guess now it would be. But I've always liked kids. It was nice to see the younger kids smile, as well as receive compliments from adults. My Magic is pretty rare in my area. So, it became a huge part of my identity. I just hope my new Magic treats me just as well."

"What about girlfriends?" I pry. He hesitates to respond. "You mean you haven't..." I trail off.

"No, I haven't."

"What else haven't you done?" I say shocked.

He pauses for a moment. "A lot."

"Like what?"

"Tell a girl I care for her. Which I'm pretty sure is obvious. Because I'm so—ya know."

"Innocent." I interject. "Luke, you don't have to be forever."

"I try but it's hard for me to get close to girls. Mostly because I know I'll get tongue-tied. Or that I will never be able to admit how I feel."

"Really?"

"Yep, story of my life."

"Maybe—I could help?" I say.

Luke 21

"How could you help?" I ask.

Is she serious? How is she is going to help me with girls, when she can't even interact with people without being passive-aggressive? As much as I'd love to say that so bluntly, I'll be polite.

"I mean, I am a girl after all." she smiles.

A *scary* one, though. Maybe if I wanted to run someone off, I'd go to her first—no doubt. But I'm still not sure why she's so *interested* in me all of a sudden. I know it can't be good. How am I gonna figure it out? She can play her game, while I sit here and play dumb. I'm sure she thinks that without my help. I just want to relax. I've been getting firewood and catching dinner for days. I'm *exhausted.*

"So, what's it like when you get around her?"

"Nerve-racking. I want to tell her, but I get all twisted and it never turns out well. Then, you know, she fills the empty air by taking over a conversation. I end up listening instead of asking what I want to say."

"Well, why not skip that part?"

"What do you mean *skip it*? There's no button."

Rhys responds, "You most likely try to greet her and ask her how her day was, and then transition into that lovey dovey stuff, am I right? Because you think that's what she wants. That right there. *Don't* do that."

"What?! Wouldn't anything other than that, just be considered rude? Not to mention overbearingly forward?" I ask.

"Maybe, but better than a pathetic babbling mess." she shoots back.

I glare at her, giving her the evil eye.

"Sorry. I can see I struck a nerve."

"Uh huh."

"But just tell her." she states.

"I'm trying."

"No, I mean when you walk up to her screw the greetings. Just say 'hey I really like you will you go out with me?'."

I scrunch my face at the thought. I'm not confident enough to do that. Most of all, I'm not Ari. That sounds like something he would say. The actual *liking them* part is up for debate.

"Do you want to get the girl or not?" she says, throwing her hands down, getting worked up about it.

When did she become so passionate about my romantic involvements? It's not that serious. *Tone it down a notch.*

"Of course I do."

"Then act like it." she continues, "While you're sitting here figuring out how to save the world and ask a girl out, she's probably falling for some other dude. Doing God knows what."

"I doubt that, on many levels."

It's *Sandra,* after all. She's level-headed and calm. The type to think things through. She's like me. People like us don't do things *just because.* We do things because we have to, or because we want to. She may be in a league outside my own, but that much is true. At the end of the day, we're all similar people.

Well everyone except Rhys. At the moment, I can't see her as anything but an aggressive, dominant, secretive, bossy, total *nut.*

"I'd beg to differ." she smiles.

Does she know something I don't? What is she getting at? Rhys doesn't smile, so that means something is up.

"Enlighten me." I say, curiosity piqued.

"All I'm saying, is that no woman—no matter who she is—is going to sit around forever waiting for a nice guy to come along. They'll eventually move on from whomever they're waiting for, or some other guy might snatch them. And the other person may not be as nice."

"I see."

She shrugs her shoulders, "Just saying."

"How do I know if I've lost her?" I ask.

"Trust me, you'll know. You'll feel it."

"Listen, I know you're trying to help and all. This advice is great for someone who could pull it off, but I'm not that type of person. Is there anything else? Another way?"

"Well—I guess there is one other way you could tell her." Rhys responds.

"I'll take anything else but *that*."

"I don't know…it takes a second of boldness."

"A second I can manage. That's a whole sentence. Well—we've seen were that's gotten me."

"This method is quite different than the others."

"Good."

Rhys grabs and kisses me.

Ari 22

"Sandra, what have you been doing upkeeping base this entire time? You're a natural at shooting. Maybe an even better shot than Rhys!" I laugh.

"No no. I'm decent. I don't need to be good at it any more than I already am. Plus, I'm sure once we're out of here, it won't serve a purpose anyway."

"If you say so." I say as we walk towards camp, moving branches to the side as we walk.

"It's not a big accomplishment. It's just a small rabbit. Poor bunny." she glances at her kill, making sure to hold it a good distance from her body.

"It was a small *moving target.* If you can do this with a makeshift bow, I don't want to know what you can do with a *real one.*"

"Is that so?"

"Yep."

I feel my stomach drop suddenly—stopping me in my tracks. There's no threat approaching us. Nothing's changed. But my gut feeling, my intuition, is telling me there is something wrong. I don't know what it is. What am I supposed to do with this feeling? Why warn me now?

"Is something wrong? You stopped." Sandra whispers.

"Huh—" I shake my head, "No, I'm fine. I'm sure it's nothing."

We keep walking a bit further and reach camp in no time. The strange sensation gets worse. Like *something* is trying to prepare me for a bad situation or encounter. A gut feeling. Who did we leave out there? Luke is usually out all day; I didn't bump into him on my hunting trip. Which is odd, because we make it back together near the same time. I remember leaving Rhys here.

Oh no. *Luke and Rhys.*

I run over to Rhys's tent and kick it, sending it flying into the bushes behind it. Revealed are the two of them, kissing. Anger riddles Rhys's face.

"What the hell Ari?! That was my tent!" Rhys yells.

"Seriously." Is *this* what my gut wants me to find?

I pull Luke up by the collar. He stumbles to his feet. My body is raging.

"What are you *doing*?"

"More than you, apparently." Rhys says, eyeing Sandra.

"I *told* you I had that handled. There was no reason to drag Luke into this mess."

"Maybe had you acted a little faster this wouldn't have happened at all." she points out.

I hear Luke in the background apologizing to Sandra for having to see that. Though I'm positive Sandra doesn't understand the full extent of his apology.

"Don't apologize." I say to him.

"Yeah," Rhys agrees, "there's nothing to apologize for after all. What's there to feel guilty for? I mean Ari and Sandra slept together."

"What..." Luke gasps in shock.

Sandra's face blushes red at Rhys' reveal. She covers her face with her hands. It's not exactly a crime, she knows that. But it's not something you want to be aired.

"Rhys!" I yell at her for crossing a line.

"What?" she says unapologetically, "It's no different than what you did with Sandra."

"You don't even like Luke!" I scream.

"What—are you going to tell me that you love Sandra?"

I stand there looking at her, unable to answer. It's not because I don't have an answer, it's that there is no reasoning with Rhys. She doesn't get it.

Yes, I've slept with women from all walks of life. Consensually. They were usually new to the houses they work for. So, what can I say? Sandra was just a notch on the belt?

"Well then?" she smirks sinisterly, "Remember: had you just done what you said you would sooner, we wouldn't even be here right now. Luke wouldn't have been left in my hands."

"Okay everyone, just calm down." Sandra says as she walks up to Rhys and I.

"I said I would."

"Yet you still haven't"

"I told you..."

"Then just *do it already!*"

I pull Sandra in front of me by her wrist. I grab the sharpened bear tooth from my pocket and stab her from behind till it pierces through her heart, as far as it can go.

"*I'm sorry...*" I say barely above a whisper.

"Ari!" Luke screams.

She gasps in pain. Her blood pouring onto my hand. It stains not only my hand, but my memory. I yank the tooth out of her. She stumbles forward, trying to breathe. One more death I've caused. Another bloodbath at my feet.

Luke started to run toward Sandra when her whole-body catches fire and she begins screaming. She's being *burned alive*. She rolls around on the ground in agony. We're unable to touch her. We can't save her.

The flames transition from red to blue. Embers flicker wildly. Smoke rises. *Rhys* is making the flames *hotter*. Sandra is coughing and gagging, spitting up blood. She clutches her heart.

"Somebody—help me!" she screams.

"Rhys!" I bark clenching my fist.

"What?"

"I—"

"Wounded her. But she's not dead."

"Rhys stop it!" I yell.

"Oh, so you do care for her then. *That changes everything.*"

The flames grow higher and becomes a pure bright white. Too blazing to look at. Sandra screams at the top of her lungs in torture. I dare to look at her through the intensity of the flames. When I see her face, I can tell that she's crying. But the tears just burn right off.

Save her, I think to myself.

I can't. No more than I could save my own mother when she died. I can't save anyone. Not even myself.

"Please—Rhys stop." I say begging, watching someone's inevitable death becomes too much to bare.

"No."

Luke 23

Sandra's body is covered in burnt blood and charred skin. The oxygen, the *life*, has been sucked out of her.

"No, no, no," I repeat, "I can save you. I know I can."

I put my hands above her body and think about the rabbit I healed. A yellow light begins to emit from my hands. So it *has to be* working—yet I don't see her mending.

Healing her should be *easy*. I healed the rabbit involuntary, what's different now?

Work got damn it. It has to.

Still no sign of recovery.

"No, it has to work." I say to her.

"Luke, it's fine."

"Don't say that!" I yell at her.

"Luke..." she trails off.

Her head falls to the side and her body lays on the ground motionless. I involuntarily stop conjuring Magic. She can't be dead. She wouldn't go out like that.

Wake up. wake up. Nothing. Her eyes become glassy. They hold no emotion.

Sandra.

"She's gone." I whisper as I close her eyes.

I pick Sandra up off the ground, holding her in both hands, heading to her tent. The limpness of holding her arms hits me hard. I inhale and exhale deeply, trying to keep myself together.

"What are you doing?" Rhys asks.

"Taking her body to her tent."

"What's the point? Leave her there to rot in the dirt."

"I wish I could leave *you* to rot in the dirt." I shoot back at her, "I'm sure her family would like to have a body for the funeral. Even you as a Royal should understand that." I say glancing over my shoulder.

Ari looks down at the ground when he hears that. Is it possible regret? Grief—even though he caused this? There is no point in asking. The only thing I can truly care about right now is Sandra. She's my priority. There's plenty of time to hate the world and *these two* later.

I carry Sandra's body to the tent. I kneel inside and lay her body down. For all the pain she just endured, she looks peaceful, graceful somehow. Then again, I'm sure that's how she always wanted people to see her. A Queen. Nothing more, nothing less. I'd say her mission was accomplished.

Exhaling slowly, I begin to talk to her, "You know, all this happened really fast. Especially for you and the circumstances you came under. But I hope you don't mind me talking to you. It's a common belief in Delnari that the soul still lingers for a few days after the person's passing."

I drum my fingers against my leg. I take in another sharp breath. Doing this is a lot harder than I expected to be. How do people do this? It's impossible.

"I'm sorry," I continue, "I couldn't save you. I couldn't even tell you I liked you, for goodness sake. Now I'll never get the chance to. I'd count this but, you're not able to respond."

I reach over and hold her hand as she lies there. These are going to be the hardest words I've ever said and the toughest thing I've ever done.

"I'm sorry your wedding was interrupted. More importantly, you couldn't do what you wanted," I whisper, "By that, meaning being able to be with the one *you* were so in love with. I'm sorry—because no one else is going to apologize to you for it. So on behalf of the universe, I'd like to do so."

I remove my hand. At this moment I'm prepared to take a moment of silence. But what's a moment of silence when Rhys and Ari are still arguing outside, tearing up their vocal chords? They could argue through an apocalypse. I try to block out the sound and do a small prayer.

Ari 24

"I cannot believe you, Rhys." I say.

"I don't know why not. I've always been this way." Rhys replies.

"Why do I find that hard to believe?" I laugh, disbelievingly.

"What? Do I really have to spell it out for you? Do you really not know by now, Ari?" she says as she sits down on the bench.

"What, that you're a sociopath? No, I think that's quite evident now."

"A sociopath that you're in love with, imbecile. Don't you get it Ari? Ever since you walked up to me in the Relic Center, I've been manipulating you. Are you mad at me?" she ends on a pitiful and sarcastic note.

"There's no way you've been manipulating me—and for that long." I say.

"I have." she smiles, "You made it quite easy actually; since you have a reputation for sleeping with women, it should be no surprise that I knew exactly how to get close to you." she says, now standing chest-to-chest with me.

"Really?" I ask in disbelief.

Rhys nods. "By the time you walked up to me, you did half the work. I could already tell how enthralled you were with me. You're really good in bed, by the way. I didn't know if all my tears would still work on a guy like you. I guess we both know how that played out."

"I guess so." I say, still frozen in place, not being able to say much.

"To my surprise, you took the bait quite easily. You were so passionate about killing her, in the name of helping such a damsel in distress." Rhys laughs.

"I won't make that mistake again." I say while looking away.

Rhys continues, "I would hope so. I'm sure if you think about this hard enough, you can see all the signs were right there in front of you."

I exhale deeply and clench my fists at my side. I turn away from Rhys to attempt restraining myself. I begin walking to my tent.

"How did she end up sleeping with you is still my biggest question." Rhys asks, "Then again, she was always quite pathetic all-around, wasn't she? She may have been a Royal, but she was no better than a peasant. Just another girl being a waste of space."

I stop halfway from my tent, turn on my heel and sprint. I transform into a jaguar midair, landing on her. She stares up at me while pinned to the ground, in complete fear.

I lean in, taking my claws out and press down on her throat. Can I transform the other parts of my body back to

human while I leave the paw? I attempt and succeed. I
continue to press her throat.

"Listen, we know you hated her—we get it. I killed
someone—I know that. You're a sociopath—acknowledged.
I've done a lot of things but tearing you to shreds will be
the least of my worries; another thing to add to my list. You
might not have respected her in life, but don't think I'm
going to stand by and let you slander a girl like her in
death." I proclaim.

I remove my paw from her throat and morph it back to
a hand. I glare at her with anger as she stands up and just
looks at me. I walk away to my tent.

It's weird how I can sleep with so many women, yet still
maintain a shred of respect for them. They don't get the
worst nor best treatment from me. It's as if my own moral
compass is absolutely straight in certain moments. Like it's
been triggered on an impulse. Other times though, I
wander the Earth without a clue of what passion, morality,
or dignity is. How can I hold any morals and do anything
right, if my own inner demons are at war? Most
importantly, can I fix it? Because if I keep down this
warpath, I don't how much more I can take.

Ari 25

I lay in my tent with my eyes closed and arms behind my head and attempt to relax. But how can I, with all these things happening around me? Majority of it I caused, or made ten times worse by my actions. It feels like I'm trapped in a cage with a key inside the lock. I'm so close to freedom, but not enough strength to make the key turn to unlock the cage door. I'm stuck.

I can't believe I impulsively killed an innocent girl. I can't believe I was manipulated, and I didn't see it until now. I'm second guessing everything now. Did my love back home also manipulate me? I killed for her first. Did she just need me to get rid of her husband by tempting me with money and power? It's human inclination to want those things. We are programmed that way. So, if we're programmed that way, is the urge to want money and power even worth trying to fight against? Do I even stand a chance?

I would go to Sandra now if I could, and explain this whole mess between the three of us. Why my actions were so impulsive and my constant struggle. Not sure if she'd listen or care, but things could've been a lot better had we communicated.

Or maybe not, since this all led to her inevitable demise. Everything is just a mess and I don't know who I am or what I want. This entire trip, I've been an advocate for making change and trying to do new things. Funny how I can spout that nonsense to Sandra when she came to me, but I haven't changed at all.

What did I want from her that night, anyway? She's a nice girl and she didn't ask me to do anything I haven't done before. We had an amazing time that night, and somehow, I still managed to stab her in the back. There are so many questionable things I've done, and I don't know if

I can turn back. Is it too late for my pathetic, merciless soul to be saved? Do I even deserve it?

Everything around me turns to shit. Maybe I'm better off in this abandoned forest forever. Who knows what other things will happen when I get back to the temple?

On the other hand, I already did the worst thing someone can do on our sacred grounds back home. That should be an incentive to never return; who knows what they'll do to me if they find out.

No, no, no. I can't run from my problems. I must face them head-on and attack with all my might. At least that's what my mother used to say before she died.

I miss her so much too. I used to think about her every day, giving her prayer and offerings. Then one day I fell off the wagon. Now I'm this pathetic person. She wouldn't be proud of me at all. I wonder if she'd go as far as disowning me.

I guess that's just what I'll have to deal with. Two women gone, that I wish I could get their thoughts on. Maybe this is my torturous punishment. Living a life full of regrets, with no capability of ever making a single good decision.

Rhys 26

I hear rain pouring and frog croaks in the distance as I wake up. Oh, how I love rain and gray clouds. There's something relaxing about it. Stepping out of my tent I see the boys getting their hair wet sitting on the benches. Literally just sitting with a long look on their faces.

"What are you guys doing?" I ask.

"Sitting." Luke responds reluctantly, "Would you like to join us?"

"No." I state, "We don't have time to sit around. We need food, we have stuff to do."

"I'm not really in an eating mood." Ari drones in a low voice.

"Well, we still have to solve the mystery behind the Relics. I mean, Luke still doesn't have any powers. Ari and I do, but we haven't mastered them or anything." I remind them.

"Maybe you should have thought about that before you killed our smartest member." Luke says, looking at me with empty, lifeless eyes.

Seeing them like this is just pitiful. Are they really going to sit here and let all of our hard work go to waste? We still have plenty of things we need to work on; we aren't anywhere near ready to head back to the Relic Center and give a report.

"Listen, I didn't kill her," I remind Luke, "Ari did."

"You may not have done the deed, but you gave the order. Don't deny it. You admitted this to Ari when you said you had manipulated him the entire time." Luke says with anger.

"As if he has no free will." I reply. "He could've come to his senses or backed out at any time. He should've been smarter. I said it before and I'll say it again: I didn't come here to make friends."

"What about enemies?" Ari says as he gathers his tools.

"Is that a threat?" I ask Ari. He pushes past me and our shoulders clash.

Ow, that hurt. Did he really just walk through and ignore me? How rude. He can't really be this upset when it's his own actions that got him into this mess. No reason to get physically aggressive. Though he's been getting like that a lot more lately, with those shapeshifting powers of his.

"I'm gonna go get myself some food." he calls back to Luke.

"Well, Ari's gone now," Luke says, drawing out his words, "and I don't want to be stuck with you alone, again. So, I'm leaving too."

Luke quickly disappears into the forest. Soon they're both out of hearing range. I know because they seemed to run all the frogs off. Now it's just quiet. Can these two really be this childish?

Why are they reacting like this is not something that happens regularly? They're acting as if I've done something criminal. This is the circle of life. She died like her ancestors before her. I will die like my family before me. Whether by old age or assassination, it's going to happen. So why am I being punished and outcasted for something that's completely acceptable?

How do they think all these kingdoms form? How do they think, in their pea-sized brains, that our countries expand and get much-needed resources? Someone must pay the cost for all these things. For people to live their happy, free, liberated lives. Or do they think it all just happens?

No matter. Whether they want to accept it or not, Sandra is dead. She is never going to come back, so they will eventually have to work with me. Unless they both want to spend the rest of eternity in this stupid forest, they don't have a choice.

My stomach begins to growl. It bubbles at my feeling of anger and the earlier mention of food. Now I'm being forced to compromise with myself. Alright stomach, you win. It's time for breakfast, so what do you want to catch? Maybe I'll try squirrel. Never had that before.

Luke 27

I'm crouched down low behind the wet bushes. I don't know if hiding low is exactly necessary when I'm aiming up in a tree. I must admit, I've never wanted to eat a monkey before, but I frankly don't care what the kill is right now. I'm sorry, little lemur, but you're the first thing I set my eyes on. You should've been faster.

I shoot my arrow right before it makes the decision to jump. It falls to the ground, birds disperse from the danger. I walk towards my kill when I hear a familiar voice.

"Nice shot." Ari announces.

"Thanks." I reply to Ari. "So, tell me—do you get a thrill from sneaking up on me, or what?"

"Just a little. Did I frighten you?" Ari asks.

"Not too much. I mean, it's either you or a bear. I'd rather it be you." I reply.

He chuckles briefly before getting silent. "So..." he says.

I look at him as I pick up the dead lemur and throw it in the basket. Ari and I have had different hunting grounds from day one. We cross paths every now and again, but never this close. We've never interrupted each other's hunting, either. Something must be up.

"You have something you want to talk about?" I pry a bit as I prepare my next arrow.

"Do you blame me?" his words falling out of his mouth before he can catch them.

"Yes and no." I answer.

"Care to elaborate?" he says.

I continue. "I blame you because you stabbed her. But not for the overall outcome. I'm sure you feel bad about it. I notice you looking quite down and beating yourself up about it. You at least show some regret, unlike someone we know."

"So—do you forgive me?" Ari inquires.

"Sure." I say.

Ari looks at me like a deer in headlights. He just stares at me, trying to comprehend the words that just left my mouth. Is he going to be okay? He places his hands around my shoulders.

"So why don't I feel better, if you say you forgive me?" he questions, shaking me lightly back and forth with a hint of anxiety in his voice.

"Maybe because it's not my forgiveness you need, Ari." I explain to him.

"I see." he says, releasing me, "Anyway, shall we head back then?"

"Yeah." I agree.

We gather fresh water on the way back. The day is new, but the mood and circumstances are the same. Ari retreats to his tent. I drop the food and cover it near the bonfire ditch. It seems it's still too rainy to light a fire, so I guess I'll hold off for now on food. It might lighten up soon. For now, I'll go visit Sandra.

When I walk into the tent, she's the same as last time. I guess that means Ari still hasn't come by to talk to her. The other two played quite a different role than me, though. I was just an innocent bystander. I guess it'll take a while for him to apologize. Rhys, on the other hand, doesn't care, so I don't expect anything from her at all.

I sit down next to Sandra; she's now starting to lose her color slightly. Her hair is nearly gone and lips are losing plumpness. I hope she's happy, wherever her soul is.

Examining her, I still think about the rabbit I saved. I am a loss for words. Why couldn't I save her too? I was able to save the dead rabbit, but Sandra has the same requirements. Am I only able to heal animals? What are the rules to this Healing Magic?

Again—I hear a voice in my head say.

Again.

I can't make out whether the voice is female or male, but I do find it concerning that I'm hearing it. Is it my subconscious? No—if it was my subconscious it would make sense and sound differently. This is a voice all its own.

Try. Again.

I assume the voice is telling me to heal her. I don't know what good it's going to do but I don't have any better options. I'd rather try and fail. I have to figure out my Magic eventually. This is just my luck; a voice that makes me feel like I'm going insane, and Magic I don't know how to use. I don't know if the soldiers at the Relic Center would call this progress.

I sit closer to Sandra and hover both hands above her cold body. I avoid looking at her face; it just hurts too much. I close my eyes and think about the bunny, healing, and my feelings for her. My fingertips tingle, and when I open my eyes, light emits from both my palms.

I see my Magic radiating onto her body while Magic whirls inside me. I don't see a change in her, though.

I remember I was actually touching the rabbit, so I decide to put my hands on her body.

Her eyes fly open at my touch. I fall back in shock and amazement.

There's no way this is real!

She stares at me with eyes full of life, hair full of shine, and lips full of color. She's alive!

"Luke..."

Sandra 28

I inhale a sharp breath; my lungs fully expand and fill with air. My vision is blurry, and my heartbeat slower than I remember it. Slowly my feelings come back to me, my body temperature is rising. I feel like I just slept for a *decade*.

When all my senses return, the first thing I see is Luke, staring at me in shock.

"What? How? But—" he stutters.

"What happened?"

"Well—I think I kind of—" he fumbles.

"Well? Say it already."

"I might've brought you back to life."

We both stare at each other in shock. What does this mean? Not me, getting a second chance at life. But of where does Luke stand now? No one has ever brought anyone back from the dead. That's way more than anything I've accomplished, Magically. He might be the most powerful wielder.

"Not to bombard you with questions, since you just came back and all, but do you remember anything before you—you know?"

I look around for a bit, trying to recall any information that would present itself.

"I remember—" I pause, "the story about the rabbit. I remember spending time with Ari."

"Don't remind me." mumbles Luke.

"What was that?" I ask.

"Nothing." he says sharply.

"Oh, anyway...that's all I remember."

"Hello—you *died*. You're telling me you don't remember Ari killing you? Big argument, Rhys was there, Ari literally stabbed you in the back."

When he says this, it triggers my more recent memory. It plays in my head in slow motion. All the yelling and fighting. Even Luke trying to heal me in the last moments before I died.

"I remember now. *I can't believe she did that.*"

Now that I remember this, I feel so enraged. It boils within me. Now that I remember I've died once, I will make this life different. I will make a change.

I sit up straight and look at Luke. He seems different now. Strange—I notice there is a free-forming purple color radiating around him. I won't mention it; something in my gut says I shouldn't. Plus, I don't want him to go into a panic.

I get up and leave the tent and see Ari and Rhys standing before me. I storm towards them while they're still arguing. Rhys sees me and stops arguing, her face like she sees a ghost. I notice her and Ari also have colors surrounding them. Luke runs up behind me.

I summon a black orb in my hand.

"Payback's a bitch." as I hurl it at her.

The black orb enters her freeform green aura and turns it murky. It flashes a bright green, then manifests to a corrupted black. No one else reacts to the flash of color.

Rhys's body petrifies, hitting the ground with a thud. Her eyes closed and body still. I let out a breath. I feel satisfied now. The first change in my new life: *don't be afraid to react.*

"What did you—" Ari asks. "she looks like she's in a coma."

"She looks dead." states Luke.

"I don't remember you being the pessimistic one. Don't worry, I didn't kill her. She'll wake up eventually."

"Really?" Ari says, curious yet slightly impressed by my abilities. "How can you be so sure?"

"You learn a lot when you're dead."

"Is that so?"

"Yeah."

While they both examine Rhys's body, I take a peek at Ari's color. It's a healthy solid-yellow. Do these colors mean something? I look at my own hands to realize I have no color at all. Time should tell.

"Should we move her body somewhere?" I say as I notice it's past noon.

"She suggested we leave you to rot." Ari points out.

"Well then, we'll take her advice and leave her here."

"Yep." we all say in unison.

"So—what's to eat?" I say. I haven't eaten in a lifetime.

Rhys 29

"Where am I?" I question.

Everything is black. I'm standing in pure nothingness.

What is this place? I pat myself down to see what's on me. This isn't what I was wearing a moment a go. My hair is pulled back into a proper ponytail with ringlets on the side. I'm in a royal-blue frilly dress with short sleeves. I have small pumps for shoes.

I look back up. *Holy gracious.* I jump back. *I'm in the castle back home.* I don't see anyone else, though. No servants, none of the maids.

"Hello?" I cry out.

"It's not polite to yell." I turn around to find my mother behind me.

"Yes, you must always remain ladylike." my father adds, standing to her right.

Where are they coming from? Appearing out of nowhere. How do they keep doing that? *It's not polite to sneak up on me, either.*

"Well. What do you have to say for yourself?"

"Sorry."

"Don't forget to curtsy." says my handmaid.

"Of—of course." I stutter.

"That's my lovely daughter."

Is this real? It can't be—I mean it was total darkness a moment ago. If it's not real, how do I get out?

My parents walk straight through me. They're ghost-like. When I turn to see what they are walking towards, I see her.

My sister. My identical twin sister, Taya. They hug her and give her praise. They all smile and laugh.

She flashes before me, standing centimeters away. Leaning in she looks at me with a devilish smile. Her eyes have a crazed look to them. She stabs me in the chest and I collapse to the floor.

"Oh sister, are you okay?!" she screams, pretending to be innocent. "Oh no—you're bleeding." she says, kneeling beside me now.

I cough up blood and hunks of it splatter onto her chest. There's no air. I can't breathe. My vision gets hazy and everything starts blurring together. Every time I try to correct my vision, I end up with after-images.

"You only look like me, but you will *never* be anything like me. No one cares about you. No one has ever *loved* you."

I gasp for air. What? I pat myself down all over again. I'm not bleeding anymore, and I can breathe. I'm not collapsed on the ground. No one's around.

"Hello?!" I scream.

The palace entrance room is before me. I walk out of the darkness and into the light. All of the workers appear before me.

"Welcome home, Queen Rhys." they all say with a smile.

Taya appears again. "Dad wants you. He's in his office."

What trouble has she caused this time? What am I taking the blame for? *It's not real.* It's just a *spell* Sandra cast on me. It's not real.

"Or is it?" a female voice says.

I begin walking to my father's office. Everyone whispers and murmurs behind my back. They don't realize I can still hear them.

"Poor thing."

"Do her parents hate her?"

"She's so young, can she handle it?"

"Oh, you care about her well-being?"

"No." a voice scoffs.

"I wouldn't want to be in her position."

I swirl around and scream. "Stop it!"

Except everyone is gone, and the murmurs have stopped. I've only screamed into the darkness of this hole I'm trapped in. *Am I going insane?* What type of labyrinth is this?

"No one loves you." I hear my sister's voice.

"That's not true..." I whisper.

"Isn't it?" the unfamiliar voice returns.

"I—"

"Isn't it?" she repeats.

"I—don't know." I state.

I fall to my knees in despair. I can't fight anymore. I don't have the motivation nor confidence. Is anything worth fighting for? I've lost my drive. I'm stuck in this black hole of nothingness.

I'm also nothing. Maybe it's where I belong.

Sandra 30

"So, did you guys make any more progress? You know, Magically?" I ask them.

They look at each other before answering "No, not really." they say in unison.

Ari continues, "We were busy mourning your...death." he hesitates on the last word.

"Yes, the death you so courteously caused. It's fine, though. I died, and Luke brought me back. Fully restored, I might add."

"Impressive." Ari eyes him.

"Thanks." Luke replies, unsure if the compliment is genuine.

"You actually brought her back to life?"

"The details are still pretty murky. I'm still not sure how I did it."

"How long do you suppose it'll last?" Ari questions.

"Hopefully a lifetime." Luke responds.

"If I'm lucky." I say.

"You are—" Ari starts, "you are the only person to *ever* come back from the dead."

We all let that fact sink in for a bit. Will this become the new norm? Revelations like this will be happening from now on. We sorta know each other's abilities. When we get back to our homes, however, all new types of abilities will be revealed. Then what will we be able to do? What structure will society take on?

"We are out of time. We really need to find out more about our abilities. We've been out here way too long to only make such minimal progress."

"I don't even want to think about what's going on back home." Luke says, eyes staring off into space.

"Neither do I." Ari says, full of grief.

Rhys's body begins to tremble and roll over again. She looks like she's fighting demons in her sleep. I know I have Corruption Magic; it's supposed to enhance sin and fear until you've been corrupted, depending on my feelings— and their sin. But I've never experienced the side-effects of my own Magic. So I wonder what she's going through.

Rhys wakes up in a fright. Her eyes shoot open, wrapping her arms around herself. She sits in the mud without a comment or a typical smart remark. This is not what I expected at all. She's not even trying to retaliate.

"What did she do to you?" Ari bluntly asks.

Rhys just looks at me and then back towards the ground. She opens her mouth to speak and quickly shuts it before uttering a word. She shakes her head in a no motion. We only wait briefly for a response.

"Well at least you woke up." he says.

"How long—was I out?" she whispers.

It dawns on us that she's willing to talk. Just not about the specifics of what happened in the coma itself. There's something she doesn't want us to know. Which makes me want to know even more.

"I'd say about ten minutes or so." I tell her.

"*What*?" she replies frantically, filled with sorrow.

The expression on her face reveals it was longer in her mind. Was she being tortured and starved to death in there? Did it hollow out her soul? She's acting like it is. How far can my new abilities take me? Does it fit well with the new me?

A rustle comes from the direction behind Rhys. She quickly scatters to her feet and stands in an offensive position. I've never seen her willing to do hand to hand combat. Everyone else grabs something nearby they can use as a weapon. We all look in the forest hoping to find the cause.

The driver who dropped us off appears. He's holding nothing but a lantern. When we realize this, we lower our weapons but our guard still on high alert.

"I've been sent for you all."

"Why?"

"Just doing my job. I was ordered to retrieve you and take you back to the Relic Center. It seemed urgent."

We all give him a look of confusion. Can something be more urgent than Magic as we know it? Have they gathered new information only for our ears? Have we been replaced?

"We must hurry," he continues, "we have to arrive back at the center before the horses get too tired. Trust me, you don't want to travel by off-scheduled horses."

I nod. "Let's go then."

We all follow our old driver to the carriage without another word among us. It brings me relief that I will be somewhere with plumbing and hot water. I'll appreciate the adventures and lessons this forest has given me. But I also want to see my family—after all I've been through. I wonder if the others feel the same?

Luke 31

The carriage bumbles along and we all sit in utter silence. We don't make eye contact or talk about what just happened. It's like walking on eggshells. Like the air is polluted and we just can't seem to breathe. The tension is high.

I begin to mutter. "So, what's our story? I mean, it's true we didn't solve the mystery we were sent to find the answers to. But we did learn *something*. We should get our story straight now."

"He's right. We can fight later, but right now is important. We need to be honest with each other." Ari says in agreement.

Sandra weighs in, "All I know, is that I was terrified of being seen as anything unworthy of a Queen," she says while looking at nothing in particular, getting lost in her memory.

"I have been terrified of death for as long as I can remember. I've always imagined it'd be painful. I'm afraid of what happens after, if anything at all." I state.

"Fire made me feel vulnerable and powerless." Rhys says, barely above a whisper.

"Is it me or did we all just admit our biggest fears?" Sandra points out.

"Maybe." says Ari.

"We did."

"Are you suggesting Magic is running on fear now? Just making sure we're all on the same page?" I state.

"Perhaps." Sandra replies.

"No offense, but do you have anything to support this theory?"

"In fact, I do," she begins "I met a Water Spirit. She came to me when I was at the lake. She called to me. The water spirit told me that this 'new system' was to strengthen humanity as a whole."

"You're crazy." Ari says, dumbfounded.

"Maybe." Sandra smiles, "But it's all we have to go on."

"You know that sounds *absurd*. Can we really trust a random Water Spirit?" Rhys manages to find her sass.

Ari jumps in, "Well do you have any better theories? Feel free to say them any time now."

It was clear that Ari was still furious with Rhys for everything that happened. It was also crystal-clear that Rhys didn't have a solid argument. She just sat back crossing her arms and looked out the window.

"What else did the Water Spirit say?"

"A new era of Magic is upon us."

"We're here." the driver reports.

We all get out of the carriage and rush inside. It's a relief to have access to AC again. I feel like I've almost forgotten that the concept of technology existed. Hopefully things start to look up again. I look at my arm's goosebumps from the freezing air.

When everyone has made their way into the Relic Center we gather around. The soldiers from last time are here, yet they don't welcome any of us back. Their faces seem like they are about to give us bad news; none of which we are ready to take on. We're not in the mood for another bomb to be dropped on us.

"What's the report on Magic?" one manages to ask.

We all explain the basics of our experience. Ari emphasizes the point of us not having had any real supplies to make our lives easier. Other than that, we keep the report minimum and no one talks about any romances, weird occurrences, death and betrayal.

"Wait a minute," I say, "We never sent a signal or told you to pick us up. We never even gave a progress report. We were just randomly picked up without any care of how'd we been. Which undoubtedly means you needed us to be here. Why did you summon us?"

"I was so happy to get away from there, I hardly noticed." Sandra says "Now that you mention it Luke, you're right. My father's not even here to welcome me back. If he's not here, it was more than a little spontaneous and rushed."

"Indeed," The guard says, "you all were summoned for something much worse."

"King Robert the Third. The King of Delnari—has been reported dead." the guard chokes out, "He has been murdered."

"Oh no." Sandra says.

"Any suspects?" Ari asks.

"Every Royal. Everyone that worked within the house. The authorities are looking up and down."

"That's practically *everyone*." Rhys says.

"It's a Royal. Everyone has a motive to kill one," I say.

"This is true." Sandra states, "This will take a while before any conclusions are made."

We all reflect on this new information. A King dead, *My King* is dead. A Royal's unnatural death is nothing to be dismissed; this is indeed a big deal. A war could break out. King Robert the Third was far from the nicest, and not very charitable, so *everyone* really disliked him. Anyone could've killed him within reason.

I ask the burning question: "What do we do now? How do we proceed? Now we have two very complicated problems."

Sandra 32

"Well—it is well understood that you all have been absent for a while. The other Royals do know this and are also looking into the incident first-hand. They told us that you all should return home to get readjusted. Catch up on responsibilities, if necessary." The guard says, and awaits our thoughts.

"Sounds about right." I state. "We can't help if our minds aren't clear. Not to mention: we still have to update our servants and such on how to begin discovering what could soon be their new strengths."

Rhys speaks up. "Not going to lie, but I don't think I'd feel comfortable just sitting back being an informant, and not on the front lines, putting in full effort."

"I agree with Rhys." I respond. "How could we, though? We just spent days on end, fighting for everything we believe in. We were on full alert, yet they are expecting us to go pretend like it never happened. If we're being honest, we've all changed in one way or another. So following such orders are practically impossible."

"What are we supposed to do? Split up? Is this where we all say goodbye and go our separate ways?" Luke asks.

"It seems that way." says Ari.

"Okay—even if we left this instant, and carried on with our old lives, what happens with the predicament on Magic?" Luke inquires.

The soldier replies, "Well it was said that you'd all most likely be summoned again. When they agreed it was time. This was based on your progress of running things in their absence, I'm suspecting."

"So we're their stand-ins again. Figures. Can't say I expected otherwise." Rhys mumbles.

"This is it…" Luke says, sounding sad.

"I guess this is goodbye, wallflower." Ari says, hugging Luke.

"Yep."

For a succinct moment, I 'm sad. The truth was that this adventure we had, the route we were set out on, was over. The journey ended here. No more bickering about tonight's dinner. No more late-night fire talks. No more simplicity.

Now I would have to go back to the wedding I had run out on. I'd be more responsible for Royal things, not maintaining camp and giving advice. More than just trying to keep everyone on the same page. Sure, Royalty has those jobs, but they happen on such a larger scale and adds overwhelming pressure.

In the forest it was just us; a team. Yes, we fought and killed each other. Things happened that were unplanned. But we all survived it, together. Now we'll be returning to our solitary lives as completely changed people.

Ari stands in front of me without saying a word. He looks at me, eyes glistening. They seem apologetic and unsure. It's true he was the one who killed me, he isn't off the hook by a long shot. I don't want to leave this moment rocky, however, and look back on it with regret.

I extend my arms toward him, welcoming a hug. "Fine, you can hug me this time. Next time—I might not be so nice." I take him by the shoulders firmly and look at him. "After all: I'm Royal." I laugh.

"If that's where our journeys take us, then so be it." he replies.

I think that's the first time I've ever heard Ari mostly own up to something that was his fault. He was being sincere. I guess we all really did change. He's on the path to being more responsible.

"I'll meet you all again next time. For now, I am leaving. Goodbye." Rhys talks while walking away, leaving us to our goodbyes.

Luke approaches me with much hesitation. I throw my arm around him and hug him tightly. He wraps his arms around me. Before I can think of what I want to say, the words just fall out.

"I'm going to miss you. I feel like I've known you my entire life, though we only spent about a week or so together. What am I going to do without you?" I ask.

He responds, "Keep living your life and remain the strong person I've always admired."

"Who's going to keep my secrets then?" I whisper into his ear.

"You're a Queen," he reminds me, "you can summon me for a chat anytime you want." he laughs.

I look at him with a genuine smile. The world truly needs more people like him. He could do great things in life. I hope he enjoys a full life. After all, a commoner has that luxury.

I let out a long sigh and we both let go.

"Don't worry," he says, "I'll miss you too. Believe me."

"Yeah, well I guess it's my turn to walk through those double doors. Can't wait to meet again." Ari waves, leaving.

Now it was just Luke and I in the room with the soldiers. I breathe heavily not knowing what more to say. He stares at the ground, I pretend to look around as I twiddle my thumbs.

Why doesn't he say what he's thinking? There's obviously something he wants to ask me. When will he ever just come out and say it? I'm literally standing here waiting on him. We said our goodbyes, but who knows how long it'll be before we talk again and he gets another chance.

He lets out a breath and looks at me to say "See you around."

He leaves through the double doors, leaving me dumbfounded about his lack of a question. Now I'm alone with the soldiers. That's it, I suppose.

I'm far beyond ready for what I'm about to do when I arrive home. I shouldn't think like that. I'm stronger now than I've ever been, and no one can take that from me. Not even my parents. Just because I'm back home now, doesn't mean that I have to go back to the girl I was. I am a Queen. I must act like one.

Ari 33

I'm welcomed home by the cool breeze from our mountain side. I'm slightly relieved to be back, yet still worried about my future. I walk up the stone steps to the main quarters, where we all usually gather for meditation.

I'm slowly approached by two elders who I don't really know all too well. They are wearing pitch-black robes—that usually indicates a special occasion. Other monks arrive, walking towards me in two parallel lines. When they reach me, they kneel down on one knee.

The main elder approaches me next. He raises both hands above his head to bestow upon me a little black book. It's small and leather-bound, kept sealed by a ribbon. Everyone is still silent.

A familiar voice comes from behind me. "Take it—as you are now the new head of our monastery. You can choose to lead us in a new direction and become a King, or help us walk our traditional path. The abbot chose you to decide, in this moment."

Me? Why would anyone in their right mind choose me? I get that I'm the abbot's right-hand, but why can't an elder do this? Someone more experienced. I mean, I should be the last person put in charge of anything.

I turn around to face the voice, it's Rosalind; the woman I had gone the extra mile for. The one I've loved since we met. The old abbot's wife.

"What do you mean 'I was chosen'?" I whisper.

"Well we don't know exactly what happened. He's technically missing. But you were his favorite, and the last person he mentioned before he disappeared. So, we place our fate in your hands." Rosalind explains.

Missing. So now we have a dead King—Robert the third—and a missing abbot. They might want me as King now, but what would they want when they discover he wasn't missing—he was actually dead. All because of my doing.

How would they treat me then? Would they follow my rule because it's our fate? Or would they all turn on me, because I strayed too far from the rightful path? Truth is— I'm just scared of the karma I have heading my way.

I take the black book from the elder's hand. They stand up watching me, waiting for their new orders.

This is so weird and feels so wrong. But I must do this.

"From today forward...I shall be King. Rosalind will keep her position by my side. Other than that, everything will continue as normal until you are informed otherwise by me directly." I say, hesitantly trying to choose my words wisely.

"As you wish." the elder says.

They all go back to what they were doing before my arrival. This feels wrong. Like something was out of place and not just me.

I admit that I've done a lot of misdeeds. To get to where I am today, I had to kill a King. My own leader, who had never once wronged me. Then everything with Rhys. Most importantly, I slept with a girl, knowing I would eventually kill her.

This is not only bad in itself, but now that I'm King, I'm sure Sandra and I will cross paths again. This time as equals. She can hold her grudge against me and call an order to take out my entire country, if she wanted.

She has every right to be angry with me. I stabbed her in the back causing her death. And when she came back to life, I didn't even apologize. I didn't do the right thing. I never have, and now the people I love are going to be affected from my bad decisions.

Rosalind, still hovering nearby, says "So what will you do now? We can officially be married, like we've always wanted."

She looks at me with lustful eyes. I remember them well. They are so beautiful, and she is so alluring. I've done everything I could for her, for us. Now I'm finally where I wanted to be.

"I don't know what I'll do." I reply.

"Do whatever you want..." she smiles flirtatiously as she takes my hands and wraps them around her hips.

Playful as always, just like old times. She hasn't changed since the day I left. Then again, I don't know why I would expect her to. I'm the one who left.

"I don't know what I want." I say.

I take my hands off her and walk away. I'm not trying to reject her, but I need time to think. Not about women, like I always do. But about myself, and what's right and wrong. Why do I always choose wrong even when I know better?

Rosalind stomps her foot in anger and returns to her chambers. I feel kind of bad, because she was ignored constantly in her previous scenario, with the abbot being an inattentive spouse. But this was unexpected. I thought I'd be regular Ari forever. Sneaking around with the abbot's wife. Now I'm finding out that neither of those things are true. Now I'm wondering if any of the things I had to go through were worth it.

Rhys 34

I arrive at my frozen tundra palace. I burst through the double doors and the doormen sound their trumpets to announce my arrival. My family is standing directly in front of me, as if they've been staring at the door waiting the whole time.

My mother is in a gray slim dress. Her arms resting upon my sister's shoulders. They both look worried. Did I expect something different? Maybe a little, but I shouldn't have. Expectation is the root of all heartache.

"Sister!" Taya screams, "I missed you!" she runs up and hugs me tightly. "Why did you have to come back? Things were fine without you. Decoys are supposed to die, so why didn't you choke already?" she jokes.

"Oh sister," I sing, "I've missed you too."

That's much better. This is exactly how I left home. My sister Taya having all the power, and me being her fill-in for any appearances. That way, if it any harm came to her, she wouldn't be in jeopardy. This job was hell.

Taya always received the attention and praise of a Queen. Always holding intellectual conversations about trades, always representing fiercely yet classy, always ruling with a firm hand.

Oh wait—that's me. Taya just reaped all the benefits of my efforts and appearances.

No, it wasn't enough that Taya had the real crown, power, and title. She also needed all the attention. Apparently for her, having mom and dad's attention wasn't enough. She needed everyone's. It didn't matter if it was for her safety or not. Taya was a power-hungry, two-faced, attention-grabbing monster. That is what made her so dangerous.

"Come girls, let's have some tea." Mother announces.

"Delightful." Taya says.

We make our way to the banquet hall. The dinner table can literally fit 2,000 people. Which is weird, because we never seem to accumulate that many people. Maybe in another era of our reign, but not since then.

We all take our seats and say our grace. My mother gives a rush order of tea; requesting green tea for herself, blueberry tea for me, and chamomile tea for Taya.

The waiter leaves and returns with tea after a few minutes. He brings back a lemongrass tea accidentally, instead of the green tea. Mother is furious. She throws the cup at him so hard, the teacup shatters against his skin. Hot tea and porcelain fly everywhere.

He quickly cleans it up and scatters to his feet to make the correct order. My mother tries to gather herself from acting unladylike. My sister and I don't even flinch. We just wait with mother as our tea becomes cold.

"Finally, my tea." mother says. "So—how was your trip?"

"It was wonderful," I begin, "I gained a—"

She cuts me off, "I don't care about you or your troubles. Tell me what I want to hear."

"Of course..." I say in a dreadful voice.

"Did you kill her?"

"Not exactly." I answer.

"What do you mean not exactly? What were you doing out there all that time? Your sister is endangered every second that girl is alive! Do you not remember our history with them? You are a good for nothing!" mother yells.

"Mother calm down." Taya says, cooing her, "I'm sure Rhys has a good explanation. Give her a chance to speak."

"Fine. What's the excuse this time?" mother asks while rolling her eyes.

"I killed her. However, she was brought back to life by another. A commoner named Luke Merins." I answer.

My mother stands up and slaps me across the face. Yep just like old times. It's sad that these things don't phase me anymore. I remember when it wasn't always like this. Those days are long gone.

"How dare you lie to me. You mean to tell me that a pure commoner is now a threat to this house? Bite your tongue." she says sternly.

"Listen, you don't have to believe me but it's the truth. I killed her, and he brought her back from the dead. That's just the way the world works on this new system of Magic. Our greatest fears will be our new Magic. So maybe instead of hitting me, you should be worried about yourself." I explain.

They both just stare at me. Unable to make out my next words, silence falls upon the hall.

Then I finally find the words to speak. "Maybe you were powerful once upon a time. But you better hope your precious Taya is as powerful, smart, and quick as she was before the very thread of Magic was fragmented and restructured."

"Fine." my mother says, her face shows her eagerly wanting to argue.

"Fine." I mock back, "Now, excuse me. I am going to take a bath. I've been in an abandoned forest for about two weeks, living like some barbarian. I hope you find some peace in knowing your prized pawn is as useless as ever."

Sandra 35

I storm into the castle with my muddied and shredded dress. The doors slam against the wall when I swung them open, getting everyone's attention. Including my parents.

"Listen up:" I announce, "things around here are going to be different from here on out."

"What is this?" my father utters, "You look a mess!"

"I will *not* be marrying Klaud Demetri Bo." I say, ignoring my father, "Not today, nor any other day."

"What?!" my former fiancé jumps up in shock "This is preposterous. Of course you will. We love each other—we always have."

"No, I haven't." I explain, "I never did. I've pretended and walked around here, doing what's been expected of me from day one. In the name of this house."

They both just look at me with slight fear and confusion in their eyes.

"But guess what—I just spent the last week or so in an abandoned forest with people I can't stand. I was out there, alone, with no help. All the things I've had to do prior to being sent away didn't mean a *damn thing* out there. Not my looks, my name, my etiquette. *Nothing*."

They don't say a thing nor bother to interrupt. The waiters and servants start to gather around to watch what's happening.

"More importantly: I didn't need to rely on any of you." I start making my way to the top of the steps where the seats are. "Maybe it was okay before; to sit around and look pretty. But I am not that person anymore. Before I was a princess. Now I am a Queen—married or not. I've changed, after everything I've been through. And what you have yet to endure will change you too, so be warned."

Everyone throughout the castle seems to be piling in now to hear my declaration. I hope they like what they hear, because it's the truth. Not some scripted textbook speech.

"Magic isn't what it used to be. Now you must face your fears to use Magic. Based on the universe's interpretation of how your phobia can be used as Magic, that will be your results. So you are going to have to move out of your comfort zones. Some of you will get stronger abilities, some of you might weaken. Some of you might not want to try at all. That's fine, I understand your reluctance. If anyone wants to leave or back out—do so now. You won't be punished or ridiculed. You have my word. But things will be a lot harder."

I look throughout the room and at first no one moves. Everyone just looks at me. Then they start to look amongst each other and consider their options. Then silent whispers are exchanged. That's when it happened.

A waiter put down a tray and got down on one knee and said "Long live Queen Sandra."

One by one, then ten by ten, people followed suit. They were going to stick by me. *The real me*, not the porcelain version of myself they had all known. I had been afraid they would leave, all of them. Instead they stayed and pledged themselves to me. I couldn't be prouder of not only myself, but the bold servants, who weren't just servants in my eyes now. They were my *family*. Every one of them.

My father approaches me, stopping at the bottom of the stairs. He glares at me with stern eyes and clenched fist. I stare back, firm on my position, unmoved by his gesture. He then got down on one knee and pledged himself to me.

Luke 36

I was halfway to insanity by the time I had realized what I had done. Leaving her there to wonder about what I hadn't said. Making myself wait until circumstances changed. Truthfully though, it didn't matter the circumstances, because I'll back out when the opportunity arises again. It's how I am—she deserves better.

Even if she does reject me though, I still needed to do this for myself, at the very least.

So, I told the driver to turn around, that I needed to tell Sandra something. That I needed to get to her wedding asap. This was life or death. He sped ahead, and the horses neighed. I prayed it wasn't too late when I got here.

Now I'm in front of the double doors of her castle and everything I thought back in the carriage seemed so silly and miniscule. I had come all this way to waste my time. But she's on the other side of this door and *she needs me*. I want her to know how I feel.

With those very words I throw open the doors with all my might. Everybody in the room stand and look back at me. Sandra makes eye contact with me while she stands tall at the top of their steps.

I begin.

"I know who you are—I was there in the forest. I listened to you when you needed me. And I know you are betrothed to someone else—but I have to say it." I walk to the bottom of the steps.

"Marry me."

"Are you insane?!" her father jumps at my statement. "She's Royalty! You are nothing but—."

"My husband." Sandra declares.

"What?! But he's just a commoner! He has no title, no land, nothing. He has no crown!" the King babbles.

I'm in *shock* from her response. I don't know her full story, but she's grown *a lot,* if she's standing up to him. Maybe she does have an extremely fierce side to her. More than she has led me on to believe in the forest of Oku. But it's okay, I'd stick by her side regardless.

"Then we'll *get* him one." Sandra says.

"I object—he will always be a commoner, no matter how you dress him." Her former fiancé says, stepping up next to her.

She stands face-to-face with him. She glares at him with daggers for eyes and snarls.

"He is kind, loyal, and brave. That so-called commoner has a name. It's Luke Merins. Your future King. He has done *everything* to help me and this country, including bringing me back to life." she says as she walks towards him in anger, making him retreat step by step. "If you have a problem with it—then you can *leave.*"

Author Bio

Erin McMillan, is a fantasy author who lives in the heart of Miami. Aside from writing whimsical worlds with magic she enjoys playing guitar, singing, and meeting up with her friends to play Dungeons & Dragons. After defeating mythical creatures and slaying Beholders you can find her 'tubing about writing advice and daydreaming.

Coming Soon:
Totality (the sequel)

www.ingramcontent.com/pod-product-compliance
Lightning Source LLC
Chambersburg PA
CBHW031952130726
47905CB00009BA/3012